Jo Returns to th

The Chalet School series by Elinor M. Brent-Dyer

Elinor M. Brent-Dyer

Jo Returns
to the
Chalet School

ARMADA

Jo Returns to the Chalet School was first published in
the U.K. in 1936 by W. & R. Chambers, London and Edinburgh.
This revised edition was first published in Armada in 1970.

Armada is an imprint of the Children's Division,
part of the Collins Publishing Group,
8 Grafton Street, London W1X 3LH

This impression 1989

Printed and bound in Great Britain by
William Collins Sons & Co. Ltd, Glasgow

Contents

CHAPTER 1

A Surprise for the Chalet School

The girls of the Chalet School were all in their places for the assembly with which school always began on the first night of the term. There were now more than a hundred and fifty girls, thirty-five of whom belonged to St Agnes', the Junior house; while the rest were distributed between St Clare's, as the Middle house was called, and Ste Thérèse's, the original school, where the Seniors lived, and all form rooms were.

The Chalet School had been started by Madge Bettany, now Mrs Russell, wife of the doctor who was head of the sanatorium at the Sonnalpe, a broad shelf up in the mountains on the opposite side of the Tiernsee, near which lake the school was situated. For the four terms before this Jo Bettany had been Head Girl. But Jo's school days had ended with the end of the summer term, and she was to be followed by Louise Redfield, a charming girl from one of the southern states of America. Louise felt rather diffident as to her ability to take Jo's place; but those who had appointed her felt no doubt. She was seated in the Head Girl's chair, next to her own chum, Anne Seymour. On her other side was Paula von Rothenfels from Hungary, another of the prefects. The remainder of the prefects were Thora Helgersen, a big Norwegian, who would leave at Christmas to go home and keep house for her father and brothers; Luigia Meracini, a dreamy

Italian; Margia Stevens, the school musical genius; Elsie
Carr, a pretty English girl; Arda van der Windt, from
Holland; Cyrilla Maurús, a compatriot of Paula's; and
Gillian Linton, another English girl. Gillian had only
come at the beginning of the year, but had shown herself
so reliable and steady that she was gladly included by those
who had the appointment of the prefects.

These ten people sat on one side of the dais which
filled the top of the room, the staff seats facing theirs.
The rest of the school was packed into the long forms
before the dais, only the Juniors being accommodated
with cushions on the floor directly in front of the girls
of Five A. The room rang with the sound of merry
chatter and soft laughter as the girls waited for the arrival of the Head, Mademoiselle Lepâttre, and the staff,
and even the new girls were drawn in as much as possible.

"Do you know," said Joyce Linton, Gillian's younger
sister, turning to her own friend, Cornelia Flower, "I
could have sworn I saw Jo Bettany in the distance this
afternoon."

"Guess you were dreaming with your eyes shut, then,"
said Cornelia with great decision. "Jo's not here – more's
the pity! She's up at the Sonnalpe – helping to put the
babies to bed, I shouldn't wonder. You'll be saying next
you've seen Simone, or Marie, or Frieda!"

"Talk sense! Simone's in Paris, and Marie in Vienna,
and Frieda – well, I'm not sure where Frieda is, but she
isn't here! But Jo – I'm not so sure. It was just her height,
and the way she moves."

"If Jo were down here, we'd have seen her before
this," said Cornelia positively. "You don't think Dr Jem
would let her come down *after* Kaffee und Kuchen, do

you? And she certainly hasn't been here this afternoon, because we've been about the place almost all the time, and someone would have been sure to see her and shriek."

"What is that, Corney?" asked Ilonka Barkocz, one of their circle, leaning across Joyce to speak to Cornelia.

"Joyce is going batty, I guess," returned Cornelia with a snort of contempt. "Says she saw Jo round here this afternoon."

"I only wish it might be true!" sighed Ilonka. "The school will be so different with all those older girls gone. Oh, I know that Louise and the others will do their best; but they seem so *young* after Jo, and Marie, and Frieda, and the rest."

Just then were heard the sound of footsteps coming along the corridor, and the merry chatter all over Hall ceased as the girls rose to their feet to greet the mistresses.

They came by the door near the dais, Mademoiselle Lepâttre leading and the rest following. They were a bright, happy-looking set in their dainty evening frocks, and one or two of them were exceedingly pretty – notably, Miss Stewart, the history mistress, and little Miss Nalder who was responsible for gymnastics and games.

Behind them came the matrons of the three houses, walking abreast, clad in trim nurse's uniform. The girls looked with interest at the new matron of St Clare's – a tiny woman in lilac, walking between Matron Lloyd (known to the entire school as Matey, and both feared wholesomely and beloved by all) and her tall young colleague, Matron Gould from St Agnes':

They knew something of the new matron's story. She was the sister of Dr Russell, and had been left a widow. Her elder girl, Daisy, was new at St Agnes' this term, and she had another little girl, Primula Mary, who (as she was

9

still a mere baby) was up at Die Rosen with her Uncle Jem and Aunt Madge.

But interest in Matron Venables lasted a bare moment. For, last of the procession, came a tall slim girl, with thick black hair pinned up over her ears, soft black eyes just now dancing with a wicked light, and a clever sensitive face. As the girls recognized their late Head Girl, a perfect yell of delight arose.

"Joey Bettany – Joey come back to teach!"

Above the cheers, Joyce's clear voice was to be heard: "Told you so, Corney Flower! I just wish I'd made you bet on it!"

Jo went darkly red with embarrassment, and several members of the staff choked audibly, adding to her discomfort. She had persuaded them to let her enter in this dramatic manner, though they had warned her what she might expect. But she had insisted that the girls would never be so silly, and rushed on her doom with fatal readiness. Now, even as she made haste to drop into a chair behind the mistresses and hide herself, she was wishing that she had not made *quite* so spectacular an entrance.

Mademoiselle stood on the dais, her plain, kind face beaming at the excitement of the girls, who suddenly realized where they were and what they were doing, and sat down in a hurry with mingled feelings. Then, as the noise died away, she took a step forward, and began to speak. "Welcome back to school, everyone," she said in the French that was one of the three staple languages of the school. "I am glad indeed to see you all so well and happy after your holidays. But I am sorry to have to tell you that Joey has *not* come back to teach, but only to greet you all, and wish you a happy term."

A groan sounded here and there, but for the most part the girls only showed their disappointment by their faces. Mademoiselle smiled at them again, and went on with her speech.

"I welcome all who have come new to the school, and wish them the happiness that most of our girls find here. I feel sure that they will soon have friends and enjoy our life. And now, I must speak of other matters." She paused, and the girls sat wondering what was to come.

After a moment, she went on: "As this is the term when we spend so much time over our Hobbies Club, I have wondered if, perhaps, some of you would wish to extend your usual Christmas gifts to the children of our own Tierntal, and send some boxes to Innsbruck? I have heard of a poor parish there, where many of the children scarcely know that Christmas comes at all. Not for them the sweet gifts and happiness you girls know! Not for them the merriment and rejoicings that form so large a part of our Christmas festival!

"The parish priest, Vater Stefan, tells me that he tries to arrange for Christmas Mittagessen for the most destitute, but cannot hope to feed all. As for gifts, he finds that out of the question. How would you so-happy girls, who all have your shoes or tables filled on Christmas Day, like to help him, and make gifts for these little children who lack even the necessities of life? I have said nothing of this to Vater Stefan, for it seemed to me that if you did it, you would wish to give him a happy surprise. But could you not make toys for the little ones at your meetings? Frau Mieders tells me that if any wish to make garments to send, or knit stockings, or hoods, she would teach you how to do it in your needlework classes. Would you not like to think that perhaps *one*

11

child is warmer and happier at Christmas time for *your* efforts?

"For remember; if you do it, it must be of your own free will, and in your own free time. Nor must our children up here suffer. We shall have our usual play at the end of term to provide funds for their festival, however. So, if you desire to help these other poor little ones, you may go to Frau Mieders, who has undertaken to be responsible for everything, and give her your name, and she will help you to choose what you shall do.

"Now we must turn to other things. We have to welcome our new matron of St Clare's, Mrs Venables, whom some of you already know. Also, Miss Carey has come to St Agnes' to help with the little ones.

"Finally, there are our new prefects to name. Our Head Girl is Louise Redfield, and I know we can all trust her to follow worthily in the steps of those who have preceded her – Gisela Marani, Juliet Carrick, Grizel Cochrane, Gertrud Steinbrücke, Mary Burnett, and Jo Bettany. These girls have left us a tradition that I am sure Louise will do her best to continue. The other prefects are Anne Seymour, Elsie Carr, Margia Stevens, Arda van der Windt, Luigia Meracini, Thora Helgersen, Gillian Linton, Paula von Rothenfels, and Cyrilla Maurús.

"And remember, my children, that the time is coming when some of you will hear your own names read out in such a list. If you do not now learn to co-operate with the prefects, you cannot expect that those who will then be in your present places will help you. Some girls forget this when they try to rebel against prefectorial authority. It is, as the old proverb says, 'to make a rod to beat their own backs.' As you are now, so will those be that follow you.

12

"Now, that is all, I think. We all wish you a very happy term, full of good work and good play. But before we part, I will ask Miss Annersley to read out your names and forms. Today, you may speak your own languages, but tomorrow we have our English day; Friday is French day; and on Monday we speak German. New girls are permitted licence for the next fortnight. After that, they must do their best to keep the rule."

She sat down then, turning with a smile to the senior mistress, who rose amidst the clapping of the girls, and stood smiling down at them. She was a slender, graceful woman, with glossy brown hair, a pleasant face, and keen blue eyes. She was famed for her gentleness; but report said that when she was really roused, she had the most stinging tongue on the staff. Presently she indicated that, in her opinion, the applause might cease, and the girls were quiet at once; for, with the exception of the prefects, no one had any idea what her place would be for this year.

From the seven year olds in the Kindergarten, right up through the Second Form to Middle school, and so, from Five B to Six A she went; and as she read out, "Form Six B," and gave the names of the twelve damsels who made up that form, there were audible gasps of delight, for no one had expected this. Many of the girls knew they were not yet capable of the more highly specialized work required from the top form of the school, and had been wondering if it would mean a very big Fifth Form this year. Now, here they were, Sixth Form – B, it is true; but it meant different work, and a slightly different status in the school.

Evadne Lannis and her chum, Ilonka Barkocz, hugged themselves with glee at the thought. Only Cornelia Flower looked slightly dismayed. She with Evadne, Ilonka, Elsie

13

Carr, and Margia Stevens, had formed what was known throughout the school as "the Quintette". They had all known that Elsie and Margia would be prefects, and therefore Sixth Form. But Evadne and Ilonka were a shock.

"Guess I wish I'd dug in a bit harder sooner!" she thought gloomily.

Evadne, guessing her thoughts, kicked her gently. It was true that they would be separated during school hours, but Corney must not forget that out of them they would be together. Mademoiselle might have left Cornelia over at St Clare's; but she had relented, and Cornelia would share the Yellow Dormitory with her own set, as well as two or three others who were very friendly with the five. Cornelia guessed what she meant and, being a cheerful young person as a general rule, brightened up a little.

Then Miss Annersley read the names of the four who would act as senior Middles over at St Clare's, but there was no surprise here. Eustacia Benson, Yvette Mercier, Irma Ancokzky, and Jeanne le Cadoulec were all known to be steady people, quite capable of the work.

This final ceremony over, the staff departed, leaving Jo behind, and at once the gong sounded for Abendessen, as the last meal of the day was called.

"Come and sit with us, Jo!" cried Louise eagerly.

"No; come to us!" implored half-a-dozen voices.

Jo grinned amiably. "How do you know I'm not going to sit at the staff table?" she inquired.

"You aren't, are you?" asked Anne doubtfully. "You'll find it rather dull if you do that, Joey."

"Keep calm, my child! I'm sitting at my own old table, of course – there goes the second gong! Come along, everyone, or we shall hear sweet nothings about punctuality being the politeness of princes."

In more or less good order, they marched to the Speisesaal where Abendessen awaited them, and presently the room rang with a mixture of tongues. Jo, equally at home in English, French, or German, and with a working knowledge of Italian (not to mention snippets of other tongues), was kept busy telling the girls about their beloved ex-Head, and the small nephews and nieces who lived in Die Rosen, the big chalet on the Sonnalpe, where the Russells had their home. At other tables, various people attended to the wants of the new girls, and exchanged notes on how the holidays had been spent. The Juniors would be marched over to their own house once the meal was ended; but the Middles and Seniors would all dance in the big common room of Ste Thérèse's, and on the morrow, the three divisions of the school would take their meal in their own Speisesaal. Just for tonight, however, they were all squeezed together.

Abendessen over, the girls, along with such of the staff as were not otherwise employed, enjoyed themselves thoroughly for an hour or so. Then came Prayers, and the girls departed to bed convinced that, despite the fact that the Chalet School had lost some of its best and most popular members at the end of the previous term, this one was going to be very jolly after all.

CHAPTER 2

The Twins Do It

Jo's original idea had been to stay for one night at the school, and return to the Sonnalpe next day. Her brother, Dick Bettany (who was in the Woods and Forests department of the Indian Civil Service), with his wife and children, would then have returned from Ireland, where they had been spending a month of his furlough with some of his wife's people. However, Jo was easily persuaded to extend her visit to the Monday.

"It might be as well," she said, when the question was discussed in the staff room. "I'm going to have a shot at a school story for the babes, you know. Margot" – she smiled at little Mrs Venables who was with them – "thinks it would be a good idea, since I *ought* to know something about school. Daisy would love it; and so would my Robin."

"An excellent idea, Joey," said Miss Annersley, who was pouring out coffee for the rest of them. "All the babies have always loved your stories, and it will be good practice for you before you start on that historical novel you intend to do some time."

Jo reddened. "That may never happen. However, I'm going to have a go at this. And I might as well be *in* the atmosphere when I begin. Thanks, Mademoiselle. I'd love to stay."

"Then that is settled," said Mademoiselle. "But if you go into Innsbruck tomorrow morning, my Jo, I will give you a list of various goods I wish sent up as soon as possible."

"Oh, gladly! I'll run round to the Mariahilfe and dig Frieda out, and we can shop together. They'll give me Mittagessen, and then I can get the afternoon train back. I'll be careful not to miss it, so you may expect to see me some time about sixteen or so."

Miss Wilson, the science and geography mistress, got to her feet. "You might do some shopping for me as well, Jo. It's only a list to leave at the book shop. But ask them to get them through as soon as possible, will you?"

Jo nodded, and then she looked round the rest of the staff. "Anything I can do for anyone else?"

Nobody seemed to want anything, so, as it was getting late, the meeting broke up, and Jo returned to the pretty guest room next door to Mademoiselle's.

On the morrow, she set off by the early train to Innsbruck, the nearest big town, where she fulfilled her programme to the letter. In due course she arrived back at the Tiernsee, with a new fountain pen, a bottle of ink, a ream of foolscap, and three of Miss Wilson's books which happened to be in stock.

It was not a pleasant day, being foggy and cold. Jo reported on her errands, and then departed to her own room, where the stove had been lit. There she settled down to make a start on her book by scribbling down a list of all the monkey tricks she and her set had played in the joyous days when they were Middles.

Early on the Monday morning, Mademoiselle was sitting in her study, glancing over the work for the day, when the telephone rang. The switchboard indicated that it was the private wire from Die Rosen, and she hastened to plug in, wondering, as she did so, what could be wrong, for the people at Die Rosen were usually too busy in the early morning to trouble with telephone calls.

"'Ello!" she called. "Qui va là?"

Back came an agitated voice. "Oh, Thérèse! Is that you? This is Madge Russell!"

"Marguérite chérie! But what, then, is wrong?" asked Mademoiselle anxiously.

"What *isn't* wrong, you mean! Can you possibly keep Joey for the next few weeks?"

Mademoiselle raised her eyebrows. "But certainly, ma chère. But what, then, has chanced?"

"It's measles!" said the agitated voice. "Jo's had it, of course; but there's no point in risking her getting it again."

"No," agreed Mademoiselle, though inwardly she was wildly deciding to quarantine Jo the first moment she could. "But how has this come? Jo has said nothing to me; and, indeed, I thought all the children were well."

"So they were. But Dick and Mollie and the babes came back from Ireland on Thursday – luckily *after* Jo, Daisy, Stacie, and the Robin had gone off to school! Rix had taken cold on the journey, they thought, and he was very tiresome and fretful. I just thought it was natural tiredness, especially when Dick calmly informed me that they'd come straight through from Paris – and with all those youngsters, if you please!"

"Yes – yes!" said Mademoiselle impatiently. "But I am desirous to know all about this illness."

"Oh, you needn't worry about infection," returned Madge Russell with a rueful laugh. "Dick and his family have been away nearly five weeks, and those children must have got it in Ireland – probably from their young cousins there. We haven't heard yet."

18

Mademoiselle heaved a heartfelt sigh of relief. "I am thankful to hear that, ma petite. I do not wish to start the term with measles in the school."

"No need to fear it – from here, anyhow."

"No. Then tell me the rest of cette petite histoire."

"Well, no one bothered very much about Rix's cold. Even when Peggy seemed weepy, we didn't trouble. But early this morning, Rosa came to summon Mollie to Peggy, who had been very sick and seemed feverish. Poor Mollie had been up half the night with Jackie, who is teething, and takes care everyone shall know it. Jem wasn't in, of course – he never *is* when he's specially wanted! – but she got up, and went along to the night nursery. Peggy was very poorly, and her temperature was soaring. Mollie got frightened, and came for me. Luckily, Sybil has never been near the twins, for I was afraid of Rix's cold. Jackie has been kept from them, too, since they arrived. But David and Bride have been with them all right."

"Oh, ma petite! I am grieved to hear that! And the little Primula Mary?"

"Mercifully, she'd gone to bed before they came on Thursday, and when we saw Rix's cold, we kept her right away from the nursery."

"Good," said Mademoiselle, with a thought for the new matron's fragile younger child. "But why not isolate David and Bride, too?"

"Well, Primula was sleeping in her mother's room, and we hadn't moved her to the night nursery. But the other two were there to start with, and we honestly didn't think anything of it till next day, when they'd all slept in the same room."

"And when did you discover what the sickness actually is?"

19

'Just about an hour ago."

"Oh, Marguérite chérie!" Mademoiselle's horror sounded in her tragic tones. "What an affair!"

"Yes – isn't it? Jem has sent for Nurse – *our* dear woman, you know – and he says Jo must not come back. Grown-ups always take measles badly, it seems. So that's the position. The thing is, can you keep her? If not, she can go to Gisela."

"We shall be delighted to have her," said Mademoiselle. "But tell me, Marguérite, are the twins seriously ill?"

"Peggy has a high temperature which is alarming. Rix is mainly crotchety and whiney. But isn't it appalling? David and Bride are certain to get it; and we can't be *sure* about Jackie."

"I am so sorry," said Mademoiselle. "Still, how thankful you must be that the little Primula is likely to escape."

"More than thankful," Madge Russell's voice assured her.

Mademoiselle nodded. She knew, only too well, that Primula Venables was exceedingly delicate, with very little strength to fight any illness.

"Thérèse, are you still there?"

"But yes, chérie. What is it?"

"Look here! I think you'd better let Jo speak to me herself. Otherwise, she'll be coming off up here as fast as her feet can carry her, and I don't want her. I simply can't do with her!"

"Very well, mignonne. I will say nothing until Frühstück is ended. Then I will bring Jo here and say that you wish her to telephone you, and she will obey you as always."

"That's all very well," sighed Madge Russell. "But Jo is grown up now, ridiculous as it seems, and I'm not her mother – only her sister. But I won't have her here – that's final! If she does come up, she'll simply have the pleasure of walking straight back again. Mercifully Jem will back me up, and she *is* afraid of annoying him. He can be nasty with her when he likes, fond as he is of her."

The gong rang just then, and Mademoiselle rang off with an admonition not to worry, and hastened away. She had no time to think things out. She must go to the Speisesaal, where the girls would be awaiting her. During Frühstück she might be able to think of some way in which she could help; but it was going to be difficult.

When the meal ended, and as Jo was about to follow the Seniors from the room, the Head touched her on the arm. "Jo, please go to the study; I wish to speak with you a minute."

Jo was no longer a schoolgirl, but she was still very near her school days, and the request made her search her mind uneasily for any misdemeanours as she went along the corridor to the Head's room.

"It's perfectly asinine of me!" she thought as she stood by the desk, waiting for Mademoiselle. "I'm not even at school now; and if I was, I never got into trouble quite so early in the term as this – not even in my worst days as a Middle."

At this point in her reflections Mademoiselle came in quietly. Jo heard her, and started guiltily, the warm colour flooding her clear skin. The Head realized her frame of mind, and laughed softly. "Ah, no, my dear Jo," she said as she motioned the girl to a seat. "I have not bid you come here for a scolding. You are no longer a Chalet girl."

"Oh yes, I am!" said Jo quickly, as she sat down. "I'll never be anything else, Mademoiselle. Even when I'm an old lady with white hair, telling all my great-great-nieces and nephews all about my wicked deeds. I'll never count myself as anything but a Chalet School girl."

"Well, shall we say that you are no longer under my jurisdiction? That will meet the case, I think. But you are wondering why I bade you come. The reason is, my Jo, that Peggy and Rix have caught measles, and our dear Madame does not wish you to return to Die Rosen until all fear of infection is over."

"Oh, what nonsense!" cried Jo. "As if I'd leave Madge and Mollie with all those babes and measles! Of course I'm going at once! The sooner the better!"

She jumped up, and was making for the door, when Mademoiselle's voice called her back. "And your sister's message, my dear Jo?"

Jo turned irresolutely. "Madge knows I'll go up at once. In any case, she's got Sybil to think of. She won't be able to do much herself as long as Baby's depending on her."

'Dr Jem has brought in Nurse Martin to see to the children," said Mademoiselle. "And he has forbidden your sister and Mrs Bettany to go near them. But the point is, Jo, that our dear Madame wishes you to ring her up now that she may speak with you herself, and tell you of her wishes. I will return presently, but I must seek some books from the library." She left the room, closing the door, and Jo marched over to the telephone, and got the private line to Die Rosen.

Her sister's voice answered her. "Is that you, Joey?"

"Yes; it's me. Look here, Madge, what is all this rot about my staying down here? I've *had* measles. You can't get it twice."

"Oh yes, you can, my child. I've had it twice myself.

22

In any case, we don't want any more invalids than we can help. Peggy is pretty bad, poor kiddy; and Rix is the limit! He's fretful and tiresome, and is inclined to lead everyone a dance. Luckily, he's rather scared of Nurse – or so she says – so he's behaved a little better since she arrived. But Peg is running a very high temperature."

"Poor little Peg! What about the other babies, Madge?"

"Quite all right so far. It couldn't show itself so early, anyway."

"When did it begin?"

"Jem says Rix and Peggy must have had it on them when they left Ireland. It's pretty awful! Goodness knows how many unfortunate children they may have infected! The rash only came out this morning, or we might have guessed sooner. Luckily, they've both been so poorly, that they haven't been so very much with the other children. And Primula Mary is at the Annexe for the weekend, and is well out of it."

"Thank goodness for that!" ejaculated Jo. "How is Mollie taking it?"

"As calmly as Mollie takes most things. She says that all children have to have it, and they might as well get it over before they go to school. Jem tells her that's false logic, and there should be no need for children to get anything if they're properly looked after."

"Is he worried about Peggy?"

"He doesn't like her temperature. But the rash is out; and she's got a tough little constitution. Don't worry about her, Joey. Those twins are a sturdy pair, you know. They haven't ailed since teething. The babies are the real worry, since Primula Mary is out of it. Jackie was in contact with the twins throughout the journey, and I don't see how he can possibly escape it. I don't want the worry with Sybil

23

either – especially when she's beginning with her teeth."

"I see. But look here, Madge; I'm sure I'd better come back. I don't see how ever you are going to manage with all the babes and me not there."

"I can manage very well. I *forbid* you to come here, Jo, till I give you leave. Understand that!" Madge's voice had taken a sharp tone, and Jo knew better than to argue the point any further. Besides, she was well aware that her brother-in-law would most certainly back up his wife; and though they were exceedingly fond of each other, there was one side of his character that inspired Jo with whole-some awe.

"All right," she said meekly. "If they can keep me here, I'll stay. If they can't, I'll go to Frieda for a few days. They asked me when I was down on Saturday. Don't worry about me, Madge. I'll be good!" Then her voice changed as she asked anxiously. "What about my Robin?"

"Quite safe, so don't worry. She had gone back to the Annexe before Dick and his family came back. As far as measles infection is concerned there's nothing to worry over. She's never been near it."

"Oh, Madge, I'm so thankful for that!"

"So are we all. Now I must ring off. I can hear Sybil howling for me. Ring me up at this time tomorrow, Joey, and I'll give you the latest news."

"Right-ho! Give the family my love, and say I hope that Peggy will be all right soon. Goodbye!"And Joey rang off.

She left the telephone, and went to look out of the window at the flower garden where asters, late-blooming roses, and dahlias were making all things gay. She dropped down on the broad window seat, and gave herself up to her thoughts.

"What awful luck this is! Here I thought I'd finished with school, and now the twins have let me down like this! Wait till I get hold of them! One thing," and her face grew very tender, "the Robin is safely out of it. I think I really couldn't have obeyed Madge if *she* had been in any danger."

Her splendid eyes grew misty at the thought.

With the memory of the exquisite little face, framed in its short thick crop of black curls, floating before her mind, Jo felt suddenly sick at the thought of how nearly the Robin had been exposed to infection. It was, perhaps, as well that Mademoiselle came in at that moment, having secured the books she wanted.

"It's no good, Mademoiselle," said the girl, looking up at her with a smile. "They won't have me there at any price. Can you put up with me for a week or two? I shall probably go down to Innsbruck at the weekend, if you don't mind. Frieda asked me, and Madge said I could always go there whenever I liked. So may I write and tell them to expect me?"

"But yes, dear child; certainly," said Mademoiselle. "And have you any news of the little patients now?"

"Rix seems to be more cross than ill," said Rix's aunt. "Peggy is pretty bad, I'm afraid."

"Well, my Jo, it is almost time for Prayers, so I must go. Will you sit here? Or do you prefer your own room? There is a steady table there if you wish to write. Au revoir; I shall see you at Mittagessen."

"Thank you, Mademoiselle," said Joey. "And if it's all right, I think I'll go to my own room."

"Do not forget that you must come down at eleven for cocoa and biscuits in the prefects' room. Or would you prefer that I send it up to you?"

"Certainly not!" gasped Jo with horror. "I'll join the others, of course. I'm not so sure," she added laughingly as she held the door open for Mademoiselle, "that I mayn't get bored with things and come back to lessons if the staff will have me."

"Come by all means," said Mademoiselle, wicked laughter in her eyes. "I believe Six A have algebra this morning with Miss Leslie, and your algebra was never your strongest point, my Jo, so come by all means!"

Jo had no more to say. Mathematics was her weakest subject. She hated it in its every form, and only the term before, Miss Leslie, the mathematics mistress, had vowed that the one thing that worried her was Jo Bettany's ideas on the subject. Whatever classes Jo might attend, she was firmly resolved to keep clear of Miss Leslie and all her works – in school time, at any rate. Out of school, it was very different.

She went upstairs to begin on her book in good earnest. "But oh, those twins!" she thought as she opened her door. "They've certainly done it for us this time!"

CHAPTER 3

Joey's New Discovery

Joey, being Joey, never did anything by halves. Having decided to try her hand at writing a school story, she settled down to it in earnest. She found it difficult to evolve a plot to suit her. Several ideas she cast aside as having been "done to death". Others were too elaborate, and she had sense enough to know that she was too inexperienced to untangle anything too highly involved.

"Besides, I don't believe people of Robin's and Daisy's ages like things that are all muddled up," she thought. "And I must try to keep the number of characters down, or kids will get confused trying to sort them out."

Finally, she decided to write down events as they occurred to her, and let the story tell itself. That being settled, came the pleasing task of selecting names for her characters, and she revelled in it. When her small niece Sybil had been born, Jo had been very anxious that the baby should be baptized Malvina. However, the idea had been laughed to scorn. She had had no chance of choosing for any of her brother's children since, by the time the news of their arrival came, the baptisms were over. But now she had a free hand, and she made up her mind that her heroine should be Malvina – Malvina Featherstone. Malvina's friend was to be Flavia Meredith – Joey scorned plain names, as most very young writers do – and the villain was Rosetta Fernandez. Having got so far, Jo took up her new pen, filled it, and wrote "Chapter 1" at the head of her paper.

27

"What on earth can I call my book?" she ruminated when she had done that.

Nibbling the end of her pen, she revolved sundry titles in her mind, finally hitting on *Malvina Wins Through*, which would not tie her down too much, and had an attractive sound. She took another sheet, scribbled the title in the middle, and then, casting it aside, set to work to introduce Malvina, Flavia, and Rosetta, and sundry other folk as well, to her public-to-be.

By the time Friday afternoon had ended she had done seven chapters and her story was well on its way. Malvina proved to be a most alluring person, with all the virtues that were ever known. Rosetta was certainly one of the most unpleasant little wretches that ever came to life in the brain of an author. Privately, Jo was beginning to feel uneasy about her. Surely no girl ever lived who was capable of such wickedness! And Flavia was a delightful creature – and the only one of the three at all true to life, though Jo had not yet grasped this fact.

In short, Jo was completely wrapped up in her own creation, and, consequently, became trying to live with. She was so abstracted that half the time she didn't listen to what was said to her. The girls declared that Joey wasn't half as much fun as she had been last term, and if this were the result of her giving up lessons, the sooner she came back to them the better!

The only time when she really did wake up to everyday life was after Frühstück, when she rang up the Sonnalpe each morning, and had a short conversation with her sister. Once her mind was relieved for the day, Joey retired to her room and her work, and became the complete author. She had already rescued Malvina from one wicked plot of Rosetta's (which aimed at proving the heroine to be in the habit of smuggling sweets into school and eating them in bed); had sent her flying for the doctor on her bicycle when the Head had a stroke (thus undoubtedly saving that lady's life); had caused her to be the means of saving the honour of the form in an inter-form tennis match; and was now engaged in causing her to be enmeshed in yet another plot of the wicked Rosetta (which sought to prove her a user of cribs).

This was the point at which Joey began to wonder about her villain, for even the worst girl she had ever known had been an angel of light compared with this creation of hers.

"I wonder if she's *too* bad?" she thought anxiously as she read over the last chapter she had written.

She was to be left in no doubt. Just as she finished – shortly after fifteen o'clock (three, by English time) – there came a brisk, imperative knock at the door, followed by the person of Matey.

Matron Lloyd had been at the Chalet school for nearly six years, and during that time she had come to know Jo and all her clan pretty thoroughly. When, therefore, she observed how peaky the girl was looking, how she seemed to be always wool-gathering, and what a poor appetite she had, she was determined to act.

Joey heard the knock and absently responded, "Come in!" She had no idea that the dogs of war were about to be let loose on her.

The door opened, and in walked Matron, looking fresh and crisp in her clean uniform. "Now, Jo," she said briskly, "listen to me a moment, if you please. I want to know why you ate nothing at Mittagessen."

Jo turned dreamy eyes on her. "Mittagessen?" she repeated vaguely. "Oh, am I late? I'm awfully sorry, Matey."

Matron took her by the shoulders and shook her. "For pity's sake, Jo, wake up! It's nearly time for Kaffee und Kuchen. Mittagessen was over more than two hours ago. Give me your wrist."

Jo stretched out a slim hand, the colour flushing her cheeks faintly. Matron took her pulse, then demanded to see the girl's tongue. Thereafter she turned an eagle eye on the closely written sheets of foolscap that littered the table.

"What's all this?" she demanded.

The pink in Jo's cheeks deepened to crimson. "It – it's only a story I'm writing," she said guiltily.

"May I see it?" Matron stretched out her hand.

She was not exactly the reader the girl would have chosen but Jo was not yet sufficiently emancipated from school to refuse her. She handed over a bundle, neatly clipped together at one side, and Matron dropped into the nearest chair, and plunged into the story, skimming the sheets rapidly. Jo watched her with misgivings. She knew that, whatever happened, she would get the truth and nothing but the truth – and the truth might not be palatable.

What it was to be, she soon found out. Matron, having glanced through the final sheet, laid the bundle down, a queer smile hovering round the corners of her mouth. "So *this* is why you've been so tiresome these last few days!" she said.

Fully awake now, Joey began to protest. "Oh, Matey! I'm sure I haven't been tiresome! I've kept the thing up here, and I haven't talked about it to a single person – not one! You're the very first to see it."

"I'm glad to hear that," said Matron composedly.

"Why?" demanded Jo defiantly.

"Because in a few weeks' time you would hate to think that anyone else *had* seen it."

"I'm sure I shouldn't! Anyhow, it's only meant for the Robin and Daisy Venables!"

"Then you ought to be ashamed of yourself for giving them such ideas!"

Joey gasped. "*What* ideas?"

"Such ideas about girls. Did you ever, in all your life, meet anyone as bad as that Rosetta Fernandez creature you've written about? Now don't answer me yet. Take a minute or two and think about it."

Accustomed to knuckle down to Matron, Jo did as she was bidden.

"Well?" demanded the school tyrant when she judged that the girl had had sufficient time for reflection.

"Well – er – no; not quite. But that's only to make the story."

"Do you want to write rubbish – or something that a publisher *may* – I only say 'may,' mind you – be induced to accept?"

Jo refused to answer this, but her scarlet cheeks were reply enough.

Matron went on. "If you want to publish, Jo, take my advice, and keep your characters as close to life as possible. No one is ever without *some* redeeming point. It would be a sad lookout for us if it were not so! And, in any case, no child of fourteen ever was the abandoned little wretch you've made your Rosetta. According to you, she's not only a liar, but she cheats, steals, makes mischief, and is apparently without either morals or manners. Do you *want* the Robin and Daisy to think such girls exist – now *do* you?"

"No-o-o," said Jo, very low and ashamedly.

31

"And then, Malvina! Such a plaster saint of a girl would aggravate anyone into thinking, 'Well, she asks for her troubles, and she jolly well deserves them!' " Matron smiled as she brought out the slang. Then she sugared the pill. "You've managed Flavia and that Head Girl of yours very well. I can see them; they're real people. But Malvina and Rosetta never lived outside the pages of the sort of school story with which *we* used to be bored when I was a girl – and rather worse than some, at that!"

"I – I *was* beginning to think that perhaps Rosetta was a little overdrawn," confessed Jo, nevertheless feeling her self-respect returning at Matron's approval of two of her characters.

"Overdrawn? I should think she is! And just remember this, Jo. Your gift was given you to help your fellow-men, not to hinder them. You won't help if you give them people so bad that they're either comic or irritating. I don't see why you shouldn't write school stories – and publish them, too. But tear up this rubbish, and begin again."

"Oh, Matey! I've put in hours of work on it!" pleaded Jo, clasping her manuscript as if it were a baby.

"The worse for you, then. This won't *do*! Begin again, my child, and just remember the old rhyme:

> There is so much good in the worst of us,
> And so much bad in the best of us,
> That it ill behoves any of us
> To talk about the rest of us.

Apply that to your people, and you ought to write something that some kind publisher may accept."

"D'you really think so?" queried Jo, half-rapturous, half-doubtful.

"Shouldn't say so if I didn't. And now, I'm going to confiscate your paper, pen, and ink till after the weekend, and you can put on your blazer and go and do some errands for me at the Post. I want stamps, and oranges, and one or two other items. Get ready, and I'll bring the money." And gathering up the bundle of foolscap, the new pen, and the fat bottle of ink, Matron stalked off. She turned back at the door, however, to add, "And while I think of it, you'd better ring up the Mariahilfe and tell them you'll be down for the weekend after all. You ought to be ashamed of yourself for disappointing Frieda as you did!"

Jo had nothing to say for herself. She had felt conscience-stricken at the time when she had rung up Frieda Mensch to tell her that she couldn't possibly get down to Innsbruck for the weekend as had been arranged. Now Matron was going off with her tools, and she had no means of getting any more paper in Briesau. She might as well go.

Having settled Jo, Matron finally departed, and when she came back, it was to find the table cleared of its litter, and the room looking orderly for once. Not that Jo had followed her advice and torn up the book. She could not quite bring herself to do that – yet. But Malvina and all her clan were tucked away under Jo's blouses in the bottom drawer of the bureau.

"You can go to St Clare's for Kaffee und Kuchen when you get back," said Matron as she followed the tall girl downstairs. "The girls are complaining that they haven't seen anything of you there this week, and that you might as well be at the Sonnalpe and have done with it."

33

"All right, Matey," said Jo submissively.

When she had gone. Matron shut the front door on her with a grim smile. "Some of the book was quite good," she thought, "but some of it was rank bad! Jo has it in her to do good work – but not if she tries to work herself to death. However, I've put my foot down, and I don't think she'll disobey me."

Once she was out in the fresh crisp air of a late September afternoon, Jo realized that her head had been aching dully for the past two days, and that she felt very tired. She went along slowly, her eyes on the lovely lake, which was a deep purple-blue. Underfoot, the grass on which she was walking was a rich green. The chestnuts and plane trees were golden and russet. Very few flowers remained in the meadowland, but those that were held up their heads bravely. Jo revelled in the autumn beauty, and pulled off her hat to let the little breeze cool her head.

Presently, her thoughts went back to her book. Since she had listened to Matron's diatribe on the subject, she was able to see more clearly.

"What an ass I've been!" she thought, as she turned over in her mind the various characters. "Malvina *was* too sweet to live! And not even Thekla – and she was expelled! – ever was as bad as Rosetta! I wonder," and she grinned suddenly to herself, "that Matey didn't point out that no school would have kept such a girl for two minutes! I think she must have said everything else! Thank goodness she came along in time to save me from making an abject idiot of myself!"

Here she was halted by Herr Braun, proprietor of the Kronprinz Karl, the biggest hotel in Briesau, and had to answer his inquiries about her family.

When he finally left her, she went on making good

resolutions as she went to the great Hotel Post, which was also the only shop in the district. "I'll only work in the mornings," she decided to herself, "and perhaps a little in the evenings. And I simply must put in some practice at my singing. Plato will go off the deep end next week if I don't. And if Madge gets to hear of it, there'll be trouble!"

By this time she had reached the Post, and she strolled into the little shop situated beneath the hotel entrance. Her face bore a wide smile for the postmistress, who knew her well, having seen her grow up from a wicked Middle to her present stage. Frau Pfeiffen was a merry-faced young woman, who spoke English quite well, though she and Jo conversed in German. That young woman got her stamps and oranges – Matron proposed to dose some unlucky people with castor oil that night – and invested in chocolate on her own account. Then, after a brief conversation which included giving the latest news from Die Rosen – Frau Pfeiffen knew them all – she turned to go. But just then, a slender girl of about fourteen came in, and stood looking forlornly round.

"Guten Tag meine Fräulein," said Frau Pfeiffen briskly. "Was ist es?"

"Oh, dear!" said the girl disconsolately. "Don't you speak English, either?"

"Oh, yes; she does," said Joey cheerfully, butting in in her own inimitable way. "And I can translate for you if it's anything out of the ordinary. What is it you want?"

The gloomy face lightened a little. "Oh, will you? Thank you so much. It's simply awful being surrounded with people who don't speak a word of your own language! I want some stamps, and picture postcards – oh, and a bar of chocolate."

Frau Pfeiffen smiled reassuringly. "All those I have,

meine Fräulein. Is it the pictures of the lake you wish?"

"Oh, I don't know," said the girl listlessly. "Anything will do. It's only to let them know where I am."

"Do you mean," demanded Jo, "that you're here alone?"

The girl looked up from the views through which she was glancing. "Yes. What about it?"

"But – why?" asked Jo. "I mean, people of your age generally have fathers and mothers running round after them."

"Well, I haven't – never had any. They died before I was born, more or less."

"But you must have *some*one," argued Jo. "I never knew my parents, either. My brother and sister brought me up. And we had a guardian too, of course."

"Oh? Well, my great-aunts brought *me* up. Only now they're both dead and my guardians are an awful, snuffy old lawyer and his prim maiden sister – both eightyish, I should think! I got influenza very badly, and when I was better, the doctor ordered me to the mountains for a change. It would have been fun with someone of my own age; but they only have ideas from before the Flood, and I got so dull and bored with it all that yesterday, when they were asleep at our hotel at Garmisch – or whatever they call the place – I just packed a bag, and left a note saying I was sick of everything, and left. I've heaps of money – I will say for Mr Wilmot that he isn't mean! – so I rang up the Tiroler Hof in Innsbruck before I left, and told them to reserve me a room. They stared rather when they saw me, though." Here she indulged in a faint grin. "This morning, I came up here in that funny little mountain train. I took the boat to Scholastika" – she pronounced it with the "Sch" hard instead of soft as the people round

36

Tiernsee always do – "and then I walked back round the lake and came on here."

"And do you mean to say that your guardians haven't any idea where you are?" gasped Jo, wild visions of a panic-stricken old pair whirling through her brain.

"No. But I'm going to send them a card now, and I did tell them in my note that I should be all right. My head's screwed on pretty tightly, you know."

The girl said all this in the same, dreary, matter-of-fact tones that she had used all along. There was no idea of boasting. Jo grasped this. She also grasped the fact that this Mr Wilmot and his sister must have been enduring agonies of anxiety about their charge, so she laid an imperative hand on the girl's arm.

"My dear, you simply can't just send them a card! You must wire, of course. They must be nearly crazy with worry about you. Give me their address, and I'll send it for you at once."

The girl looked at her with a little amazement. "Oh, I've plenty of money. I can send a wire myself – thanks, all the same."

"Then send it, for goodness' sake!" urged Jo.

"Oh, they won't be worrying about me. They're pretty placid. That was what I found so trying. They just go on the same way, day in and day out, and I'd had more than enough of it with my aunts! *They* wouldn't even let me go to the most seminaryish kind of school. I had to have a governess. Aunt Mariana thought schools were not the proper place for girls like me, and Aunt Sophonisba backed her up."

"Well, I can't help that," persisted Jo, who was nearly breathless over the names of the aunts. "If you think your guardians aren't almost off their heads with anxiety over you, that's where you make a big mistake. They aren't going to do anything *but* worry about a schoolgirl running loose over Europe, however aged or placid they may be. Here's the form. Fill it in, and Frau Pfeiffen will phone it down to Spärtz. And then, I think you'd better come back with me for the present."

"Won't your people object?" asked the girl, beginning to lose a little of her indifference.

"Not they!" returned Jo airily. "However, I'm not at home at present – I can't go home – the babies have measles! In fact, my dear, if it's *school* you want, you've come to the right place! I'm staying at my own old school – the Chalet School. You must have passed it to get here. Didn't you notice three houses linked up by covered passages inside a high palisading?"

The girl looked up, interest in her face. "Of course I did! Do you mean to say there's a school here? What a gorgeous place for it! I wonder – " She paused, scribbled her telegram, signed it with four initials, and handed it over to Frau Pfeiffen with some money. "Can you make it out? And is that right, please? I don't understand your money yet."

Jo gasped again, for the wallet was simply bulging with notes of high value, and this child handled it as carelessly as if all she possessed were worth a few schillings. Then she glanced at the form and noted the initials.

"Oughtn't you to sign your surname?" she asked. "Will they know who that's from?"

The girl nodded. "They know all right. There couldn't be another person with a collection like that! But I'll stick in 'Heriot' if you like." She took back the form and added the name. Then she got her chocolate, and followed Jo from the tiny shop, leaving good Frau Pfeiffen consumed with curiosity to know what all this meant.

"What is your baptismal name?" asked Jo as the stranger fell into step with her.

"Hildegard – Mariana – Sophonisba – Heriot," said the owner, with a pause between each word to give it due effect.

"*What*?" Jo was startled out of her manners.

"Yes – all of it. Of course, I don't use it. Well, would *you*?"

"Not if I could help it," Jo assured her. "But if you *don't* use it, what *do* you use?"

"Polly – nice, and short, and not sentimental."

Jo nodded approval. "Yes; I like that – though I don't see how you get it. And it's not so ordinary these days as Mollie, for instance. And I hope you don't mind me saying so, but what on earth possessed your people to give you such a mouthful as that?"

"They hadn't anything to do with it," explained Polly, who seemed considerably cheered up now. "You see, father died before I was born – at least, he went with an expedition up the Amazon, and nobody ever heard anything of any of the party again. Then I came, and mother died. There was no one left but father's two old aunts, and they took me. They chose my names, too. I had to be Hildegard because that was mother's name, and one of the aunts was Mariana, and the other was Sophonisba, so they just gave me the lot. They meant to call me Hildegard, I believe. But when I was little, I couldn't say it, and I called myself Polly somehow, and it stuck – though they didn't exactly like it. So I've been Polly ever since."

"I don't blame you," said Jo with decision. "Well,

Polly, I'm going to take you to our headmistress, Mademoiselle Lepâttre, and you must explain things to her. Oh, you needn't look scared. She's a perfect dear, and most awfully understanding. You'll stay at the school until she can hear from your guardians, and then she'll talk to them. You'll have to go in to lessons, I expect, with the rest. You won't mind that, I suppose?"

"Mind it? It's the one thing I've wanted all my life!" said Polly fervently. "That – and to have my hair cut off." She gave an impatient toss to the thick, untidy pigtail that dangled down her back to her waist.

"I don't think I'd have it cut if I were you," said Jo thoughtfully. "The fashion's going out. And anyway, your hair is lovely. I should think it looks gorgeous when it's loose."

"It's a sickening nuisance to keep tidy," grumbled its owner ungratefully. "And as for lovely, it's *red*!"

"Yes; but a deep chestnutty red. You be thankful it isn't ginger," advised Jo. "You might have something to growl about then."

By this time, they had reached the front door of the school, and Mademoiselle, amazement in her eyes, was in the hall as they entered. Jo went briskly forward to explain matters.

It was a full hour before the Head of the school had got all the information she thought she should have, for Polly suddenly turned shy, and it was with difficulty that they dragged "yes" and "no" out of her. But at length the whole story came out, and on Jo's assuring her that Polly's wire had been duly sent, Mademoiselle decided to send a fuller one on her own account. In the meanwhile she made up her mind to place Polly at St Clare's, where the housemistress, Miss Wilson, science and geography mistress of the school, could be trusted to keep a watchful eye on her. Incidentally, Mademoiselle gently suggested that it would be wiser if Polly handed her wallet over, keeping just the few schillings that all the girls had, and Polly was so enamoured of the new life to which she was being introduced, that she did as she was told like a lamb, and never suspected that one reason for the suggestion was to deprive her of the means of running away again!

It was now past sixteen o'clock, and Kaffee und Kuchen would be in full swing in the girls' common room at St Clare's, so Mademoiselle sent the two girls along there at once. Then, after phoning her wire to Spärtz with injunctions that it must be sent off at once, she turned to the private telephone to the Sonnalpe to tell the people at Die Rosen of Joey's latest exploit.

CHAPTER 4

Mr Wilmot Arrives

As Matron insisted on Jo keeping to her original plan of spending the weekend at Innsbruck, that young lady knew nothing about subsequent events until she got back to Briesau on the Tuesday.

Mademoiselle's wire had brought old Mr Wilmot to the Tiernsee post-haste on the Sunday. As it turned out, no one had missed Polly until the Friday, owing to old Miss Wilmot having fallen ill on the Thursday with a severe bilious attack. Mr Wilmot had told their chamber-maid to look after the child, but his German was shaky and the girl was sulking under notice to leave. She had chosen to pay no attention to his orders till the Friday morning, when she had discovered, to her horror, that the young lady's bed had not been slept in.

Mr Wilmot had, by that time, gone off to seek a doctor for his sister, who was really quite ill, and the girl had not dared to mention her discovery to the manageress of the hotel, so no one but herself knew anything about it till noon, when she had finally come to him and, with many sniffles, told her news. For some hours thereafter, he had been nearly frantic with worry.

Fortunately, Polly's wire had come just as he was about to seek a detective, and it was followed very shortly by Mademoiselle's; and the news that the child was safe in a school had soothed him a little. At the same time, such anxiety for a man of seventy-three – Polly had over-estimated his age – had not been a good thing, and he had succumbed to a severe headache which made it impossible for him to leave Garmisch until the afternoon of Saturday.

He reached Innsbruck only to find that the last train to Spärtz had gone, except one at eighteen hours which would get to the little town too late to enable him to catch the last train up to Seespitz, the station at the head of the Tiernsee. He was in no fit condition to undertake the long walk up the mountainside, so he had gone to the Tiroler Hof for the night, and consoled himself as best he might with the knowledge that at least his ward was in the hands of those who would look after her.

He had caught the first available train to Spärtz next morning, and arrived at the school about noon, at which hour Polly was out for a walk with the other girls from St Clare's.

Mademoiselle had interviewed him, and had talked to him very gravely about his young ward, for she had succeeded the previous evening in extracting from her further details of her life.

"You are very good, madam, very good," he had said, "but what am I to do? I am well aware that old people like myself and my sister are not fitting guardians for a bright young girl, but I could scarcely refuse our dear and life-long friends, the Misses Heriot. Come! You are the headmistress of a school. You must have had considerable experience of young people. What do you advise me to do? I am anxious to do my best for her. She is a dear child, if somewhat headstrong, and should make a fine woman if she is only trained right. The trouble is how to arrange for such training." And he shook his head.

43

"She ought to go to school," said Mademoiselle thoughtfully. "She needs the discipline she would have there both
from the staff and from the other girls. Could you not send
her to a good English school? She would be able to spend
her vacations with you, and I feel sure that she would
answer well to such training."

"Quite possibly, my dear madam. But the point is that
I do not know how to set about finding such a school. I am
an old bachelor, and this is the first child with whom I have
had anything to do. Were it the engrossing of a lease, or
the drawing up of a will, I could do it with my eyes shut.
But to choose a school for a girl is quite another matter."

"You must write to several schools for prospectuses,
and then, with your sister Miss Wilmot, go and inspect
those you approve," said Mademoiselle.

He shook his head ruefully. "I fear my dear Jane
would scarcely know how to decide. She is older than I
by some years, and what was correct in her girlhood must
be out-of-date nowadays. But I was forgetting. Of course!
You have a school here! You have rescued the child from
unknown dangers, and looked after her. Could she not
come here without more ado?"

The thought deepened in Mademoiselle's face. "We
are very full, monsieur. I am not sure that we could make
room this term for even one more. And, apart from that,
would you not prefer to have her near you in England?"

"For holidays, my dear madam, it might be more con-
venient, I admit. But I feel sure that if you would consent
to accept her as a pupil, it would be an easy matter to
arrange for an escort for her on such occasions. Come
now, I am greatly taken – yes, greatly taken with all I
have seen of your establishment" – he had seen only the
front hall and Mademoiselle's study! – "and I feel sure that

44

the influences at work here would be the very best possible thing for the child. There need be no difficulty about the financial side of it. I can give you bank references and any others you might desire. Polly will not be poor when she comes of age – far from it. And I am her trustee as well as her guardian."

Mademoiselle noted how tired and frail he looked after all the worry of the past two days; she felt her heart softening, though she was by no means certain that she wanted such a headstrong young person as Polly. "I am not the sole owner of the Chalet School," she said slowly. "I have a partner, and she must be consulted."

"But of course, my dear madam! By all means! But I trust you will put the whole matter before her in as favourable a light as possible. I know the poor child's foolish action must make you take a very dark view of her character. But I can assure you that until Thursday her behaviour had never caused us any anxiety. And I can see plainly that it must have been dull in the extreme for her to travel with an elderly man and woman. We are, I fear, many years from our own youth. But – but I am fond of Polly, madam; and so is my sister. We are anxious to do our best for her, only I sometimes doubt if we can know what *is* best. Two old people – living very quietly in a sleepy little country town – I fear we have forgotten that times have changed, and the progress there has been. But here, with you, I feel sure that she would be happy and well cared for, and learn lessons we are too old to teach her."

Mademoiselle was deeply touched by this speech, though she said very little. Finally, she had rung, and sent for Polly, who came with a semi-defiant air which vanished as she saw the old man leaning back in his chair.

She ran to him, and dropped on her knees by his side.

"Mr Wilmot! Have you been ill? Oh, I'm so sorry! It was all my fault – little *pig* that I've been! I never thought you'd worry about me – honestly, I didn't! Oh, please, please forgive me, and don't look like that, and I'll come back whenever you like – *now*, and take any punishment you like without a word!"

This little outburst of feeling was what had really settled it. Sitting back, Mademoiselle decided that the child might be headstrong, but she had a good heart. That she was absolutely sincere in what she said was plain to see. Her lips were quivering as she searched her guardian's worn, pale face with anxious grey eyes, and there was no pretence about her.

Mr Wilmot put out his hand and took the pointed chin in it. "Why, Polly, my love, are those tears? No, you mustn't cry. I am only a little tired. I fear I am getting an old man, Polly – an old man, now. And then my poor sister was so ill, and that troubled me."

Polly broke down and sobbed. "Oh, is it my fault? What a *beast* I have been! But I never meant – "

"Come, Polly! You mustn't cry, child. And as for Jane's illness, that was the result of eating éclairs for her tea, though I warned her they would upset her. It had nothing to do with you. Indeed, she does not know that you ran away. I – er – told her that I had a little business to transact in Innsbruck, and you would be with me – not quite the truth, I fear, but I did not wish to disturb her."

Polly produced a somewhat grimy handkerchief, and scrubbed her eyes fiercely. "I – I'm glad it wasn't me made Miss Wilmot ill," she said, with a lack of grammar that would have called down rebuke on her head at any other time. "And I *am* sorry I ran away – truthfully I am."

"But why did you not tell us you wanted more amusement than we arranged for you?" he asked, taking the slim hands in his and looking keenly into the tear-wet eyes. "I would have taken you about more if I had thought of it. But it is going to be all right, Polly. I have been asking this good lady to accept you as a pupil in her school, and if her partner will consent, I am in hopes that it may be arranged. You would like that, would you not?"

Polly got to her feet, looking bewildered. It was the dream of her life come true, but just at the moment, she felt that she must go back with her guardian and make what amends she could for having called that white, weary look into his face. She could find no words for her thoughts, so just stood silent, clinging to his hands.

"I think, monsieur," said Mademoiselle gently, "that Polly feels that she owes it to you to return with you, and show you that her grief for having – er – so discommoded you is real."

"Is that it, hey?" he asked. "Well, she must come back with me for a day or two, of course. She will have her – er – garments to pack, and, perhaps to get some new ones. But if you and your partner, madam, can see your way clear to taking her as a pupil of your school, I will see to it that she is here – shall we say next Thursday? In the meantime, permit me to give you my bankers' address, and also those of our vicar and doctor, that you may write to them."

Thinking it better to settle business matters without the help of Polly, Mademoiselle sent her back to St Clare's to get ready for Mittagessen, and then rang up the Sonnalpe. Mrs Russell considered that they should certainly give Polly a trial. Probably this freak of hers in running away was the sort of thing to occur only once in her life.

"And even if it weren't, we've had other girls do it, and they've turned out all right in the end, my dear Thérèse," she finished laughingly. "Take the child, by all means. I like the sound of her."

And so it was that when Joey returned from her visit, it was to find that the Chalet School had yet another girl on its roll.

"I liked the girl," Joey said when Matron had finished the story. "I thought she seemed quite a nice kid, if a bit of an ass. And, you know, Matey, she must have been bored to tears with her life! First those old great-aunts – who should have been pilloried for loading her up with such a baptismal name! Thank Heaven I'm plain Josephine Mary! – and then two aged people without much go in them! All that's been wrong with the poor kid is that she's wanted a few friends of her own age. She'll be all right once she's settled down and got into our ways. I must say the old lawyer sounds a duck from all you say; but you can't expect people as old as that, especially who seem to have lived in Sleepy Hollow all their lives, to understand a modern schoolgirl. I don't suppose for an instant that she'll do anything so mad as running away from here – she seems far too keen on school for that, from what she said to me."

"Well, I hope so," said Matron. "And if she's been brought up as you say, I hope she'll settle down quickly."

"She's not a bit pretty," said Jo thoughtfully, "though she has glorious hair and nice eyes. But she has an honest face, and I really was sorry for her – she sounded so utterly forlorn."

"Oh, I expect she's an average enough girl," agreed Matron. "As you may remember, Jo, I told you a few

48

days ago that most people are. By the way, you may have your paper again. But remember: you are not to write all day when you begin again. The mornings, if you like; but in the afternoons, you must go for walks, or play hockey or netball. And you can work while the girls are at preparation in the evenings. So much won't hurt you. But I must insist on your taking things a little less strenuously."

Jo grinned. "Right you are! I really will keep calm about it. And now, Matey, if you'll excuse me, I think I'll go upstairs and get my unpacking out of the way."

"Run along," said Matron amiably.

And, whistling gaily, Jo went off upstairs to unpack her case, and then to take *Malvina* from the drawer, and settle down at her table to read it with as unbiased a mind as she could.

As she read on, the colour burned in her usually pale cheeks, for, coming to her story freshly after nearly a week of not seeing it, she could grasp how absurdly unreal most of her characters and many of her situations were. Jo had always prided herself on her sense of humour, but it struck her rather forcibly as she turned the last page that it must have been completely in abeyance for once when she wrote those seven chapters.

"Of all the idiots!" she said aloud as she tossed the sheets down on the table. "No wonder Matey advised me to burn it! Straight into the incinerator it goes. I'm thankful only Matey saw it – and *she* must have thought me weak-minded!"

She jumped to her feet, the book clutched in her hand, and raced from the room, down the stairs into the garden, and to the place where Otto, head gardener on the Chalet estate, was burning rubbish in the incinerator. He looked up with a friendly smile and a salute as Jo appeared.

"Grüss Gott, Fräulein Joey!˜ You have had a happy time with Fräulein Frieda, nicht wahr?"

"Grüss Gott, Otto! Yes, it was very pleasant," said Joey. "Have you a decent fire there? May I see, please?"

He obligingly moved to one side, and she peered in. The fire was quite hot enough for her purpose, and with a firm hand she rammed down the sheets, watching till they caught fire. Then, with a nod to Otto who had been watching her performance wonderingly, she turned and left the place, feeling rather as if she were a mother who had just sacrificed her first-born to Moloch. After all, it *had* been her first serious attempt to write a book; and even now, though she could see that much of what she had written had been rubbish, still, it had been *hers*.

She went back upstairs rather more decorously than she had descended, for it was not quite time for Kaffee und Kuchen, and sat down at her table. She planted her elbows on the table, and set her chin on her doubled-up fists, scowling into vacancy with the intensity of her thought. Then she sat back.

"I'll begin again," she vowed. "I know I can tell a story, and I mean to do it. I can't begin tonight, but I shall tomorrow morning. And what's more, I'll jolly well *succeed* this time!"

The gong sounded just then, so she deferred hurling defiance at the Fates, and went off downstairs, where she was seized on by at least half-a-dozen people who all wanted to know the latest news of Frieda.

Next day, as soon as school Prayers were over, Joey dashed upstairs again to her room, and settled down – with different people, this time. She felt that she could not use Malvina and Co. in another book, so she had to evolve a completely fresh set of characters, and was soon so engrossed in her work, that she never noticed that a car drove up to the door, though she was at her open window, just above it. Nor did she hear the voices in the garden, nor the steps that came along the corridor past her room. Indeed, it was not until she came down to Mittagessen with a few extra hairpins in her hair, flushed cheeks, and very bright eyes, that she realized that the Chalet school had just received another pupil, and that Polly Heriot had arrived.

CHAPTER 5

Joey – The Author

Joey duly settled down to her new attempt at a school story, which presently was in full swing. She could not call this heroine Malvina. That had been sacred to her first shot. After much thinking, she decided on Cecily, and thereafter got on swimmingly. Warned by Matron's diatribe on the subject, she contrived to keep Cecily merely an ordinary schoolgirl, who led quite an ordinary life at school. She was making it a day-school, for though the past five years or so of her life had been spent at a boarding-school, she had had four years at the girls' high school at Taverton in Devonshire, where she had spent her early life.

For a fortnight, she revelled in her work. With a wicked grin curving her lips, she introduced a science mistress, who bore a remarkable resemblance to Miss Wilson, who held that post at the Chalet. Jo was fond enough of Bill, but that did not prevent her from using two or three of that lady's idiosyncrasies in the portrait of Miss Travers, with whom Cecily was frequently at war. Jo was not of a scientific turn herself, and Cecily was made to hate anything of the kind. With recollections of a certain fatal "experiment" of Evadne's, Jo provided a similar sensation for St Michael's High School, when Cecily nearly wrecked the laboratory in consequence of her carelessness. Further memories helped her to add a few more pranks to her heroine's record. At the same time, the book contained nothing that might not have happened at the best regulated of schools, though it must be admitted that most schools do not have quite such a spate of happenings all at once.

Then came a morning when, reading all she had done to date, Jo made the discovery that she had mixed up two of the prefects, and, consequently, must either re-write one of the early chapters, or the five suceeding ones.

"Oh, bother—bother—bother!" she groaned when she found this out. "That's what comes of being too lazy to make out lists. Well, I'd better do it now and save trouble for the future. Then I suppose I'll have to re-write that blessed chapter. Where's my notebook?"

Making out the list occupied her for the greater part of the morning, for having begun it, she found it so fascinating, that she finally made out the roll for the whole school, staff as well as girls. Then she put ticks by the side of all those who had appeared in the story so far.

"There goes the bell for cocoa!" she thought as she capped her pen on accomplishing this. "I'll get on with that chapter afterwards. But this is a sickening bore! I thought I'd have got nearly the whole of the next one done before Mittagessen."

She glanced at herself in the mirror, caught up two or three hairpins to secure straying ends—Miss Wilson vowed that Jo's head in these days was a very good imitation of a porcupine!—and went off to seek cocoa and biscuits, feeling that she really hadn't done so badly after all.

Cocoa and biscuits over, she retired once more to struggle with the chapter that must be altered, and, by dint of strenuous work, got it all but finished before the warning gong sent her flying to wash her hands before Mittagessen.

"How's the great work going, Joey?" asked Miss Annersley, the English mistress, as she met the girl on the stairs. "Remember, you've been *my* pupil for three years or more, and I expect you to do credit to me."

"Oh, it's coming on," said Jo lightly.

"When am I to see it?"

Jo went red. "Oh—give me a chance to finish it first!" she said.

Miss Annersley chuckled. "Well, don't, I implore you, mix your metaphors or split your infinitives," she said.

"As if I would!" said Jo scornfully.

There was a twinkle in Miss Annersley's eyes as she said, "I seem to remember an essay given to me in which the writer said, 'Like a rosebud opening to the dawn, the maiden sailed across the grass, casting light by her very presence.' Do you remember, Joey?"

Joey had the grace to blush again as she replied, "It wasn't an essay—it was a fairy story. And I was only about fourteen when I did that, anyhow."

"Well, be careful now."

"And I never did split my infinitives. I hate the sound of it too much, and always did."

"No, I don't believe you did," admitted Miss Annersley. "How many of us are you caricaturing, Joey? Let us down lightly, won't you?"

With a guilty consciousness that she *had* used Miss Wilson, at any rate, for one character, Jo looked hastily round for a loophole of escape, and found it in the face of the clock that adorned the end of the corridor. "Mercy! Look at the time—I must fly! 'Scuse me, please,

Miss Annersley!" she ejaculated; and fled, leaving Miss Annersley laughing wholeheartedly at her discomfiture.

"All the same," said the English mistress to Miss Wilson as they put away their books together, "I feel positive that Joey *has* portrayed some of us. Well, it may be good for us to 'see oorsel's as ithers see us.' I wonder whom she has victimized?"

Now, whether it was the result of Miss Annersley's teasing, or whether she had tired herself, when Joey sat down to work again, she found her fount of inspiration dry. She wrote five or six sheets—a whole chapter—and when she read it over, it struck her that she had never read such rubbish in her life. The prank she had meant to be so funny was merely silly; and Cecily and her companions spoke and behaved like a set of puppets.

Joey heaved a sigh, tore the pages across and across, and tossed them into the wastepaper basket— or rather, she tried to and missed so had the pleasure of going down on all-fours and gathering up the fragments, which did not sweeten her temper. "*Drat* the thing! I've a jolly good mind to send the rest after it and give up writing—at any rate until I'm older."

However, Jo had a strain of doggedness in her which prevented such drastic measures. But she flung the finished sheets into her case, shoved it under her bed, and went down to Abendessen in a thoroughly bad temper.

"What's wrong with you?" demanded Cornelia after the meal was ended. "You look as though you'd lost a dollar and found a dime. Guess you've got a bit of a temper."

"Don't be silly and impertinent," said Jo coldly. "You are getting too old for such childish rudeness, Cornelia."

She moved away, leaving Cornelia staring after her

with wide eyes and dropping jaw. "*Say!*" gasped that young lady when she had recovered from the shock of her full name. "I guess Joey Bettany's going bats!"

"What on earth's the matter with *you*?" demanded Elsie Carr to whom this was addressed.

"Jo's mad about something," said Cornelia. "She needn't work it off on me, though."

"Oh rats!" said Elsie impatiently. "Come on! Aren't you going to have this waltz with me?"

Cornelia put an arm round her partner, and they whirled out into the centre of the floor. But for once the young American was almost silent as she danced. She had known Joey in all sorts of moods, but this one was a shock to her.

Meanwhile, Joey had retired to the staff room, where she found several of the staff relaxing, and gossiping comfortably among themselves.

"Well, Joey," said Miss Leslie cheerfully, "are you bored that you are honouring us with your presence?"

"Oh, I thought I'd drift along and see how you all were," said Joey. "Haven't seen anything of most of you for ages."

"That's what comes of being absorbed," said Miss Wilson. "How's the book going?"

"Stuck for the moment."

"I believe most writers get to that stage sooner or later," observed pretty Miss Stewart, the history mistress. "Never mind, Jo. Give it a rest for a day or two, and then go back to it. How far have you got, by the way?"

"Nine chapters done," said Jo.

"But that's marvellous!" cried little Mademoiselle Lachenais, coming up with a box of French chocolates. "I make you my felicitations, my Jo! Soon it will be finished.

And then, perhaps, we are to see it, n'est-ce-pas?"

"Thank you, Mademoiselle—Oh, I don't know," said Jo; "it's only meant for the babies, you know. You wouldn't enjoy it."

"Of course we should!" said Miss Stewart. "How many of your own wicked deeds are you immortalizing, Jo?"

"None," returned Jo solemnly. "There are plenty of other people's to use." She suddenly chuckled.

"Such as?" demanded Miss Leslie.

"*If* it's ever finished, and *if* it's ever published, I'll present one copy to the staff, and then you can all read it in turn," said Jo.

"Joey! How mean of you! You know quite well that I'm leaving at Easter," protested Miss Leslie. "You'll have to send me a copy for myself—and autograph it, too. Are you dedicating it to us? You ought to! You certainly owe us something for all the grey hairs you've caused."

Jo surveyed her brown head thoughtfully. "Can't say I see any on *your* head, Miss Leslie. D'you use dye, by any chance?"

"*Jo!*" protested the maligned mistress. "I won't put up with such impertinence, even if you *are* emancipated now. For two pins I'd set you down to a page of quadratic problems!"

Jo scuttled to the door of the staff room. "Not if I know it! I love you, as you well know, but I loathe all your works. Whatever you are going to do when you are married, I can't think! You can't do the housekeeping bills by quadratics, you know."

"Indeed, I shall manage very well," returned Miss Leslie, flushing pink. "Go away, you evil damsel! Go and get on with your great work. You make hay while the sun shines, my child. You never know when you may be prevented from doing any more."

Amidst a general chorus of laughter, Jo took her departure, and, since no one seemed to want her, she retired to bed, greatly refreshed by her encounter with the mistresses. She was tired, and fell asleep as soon as she had switched off the light, and dreamed at least six chapters of *Cecily*, all of which vanished from her when she woke next morning, much to her disgust.

"I know they were gorgeous chapters," she wailed to her sister on the telephone after Früstück. "Isn't it like the thing? I might have written a book worth writing, just as Robert Louis Stevenson did with *Dr Jekyll and Mr Hyde*. Now, it'll just be an ordinary school tale—if it ever reaches completion."

"Don't you dare show your face here again if it doesn't!" threatened Madge. "Do as Miss Stewart says, Jo. Give it a rest for a day or two, and then come back to it. Or you might borrow Mademoiselle's typewriter and begin copying what you have done. Take a carbon, and send it to me. I *need* cheering up now, I can tell you!"

"Poor old thing! Those infants *would* wait to the limit of the quarantine! Well, at least they're not badly ill, so that's something. Hello! Evvy's screeching for me—I must fly. Bye-bye, and love to the entire family." She hung up.

Jo had the sense to take her sister's advice. She borrowed Mademoiselle's typewriter, purchased some carbon paper from the stock cupboard, as well as a packet of typing paper, and set to work to copy as far as she had gone. Needless to state, she kept making alterations as she went, and, as she was no expert on the typewriter, she made heavy work of it at first. The long sitting in the one position made her shoulders ache, and many a sheet

58

had to be thrown away because she had either jumbled letters, or spelt words so wrongly, that no amount of correction would suffice. But after five days of hard work, it was done, and she found that she could go on quite well. The chapter she had torn up almost wrote itself, and when that was done, another idea came to her, and she made haste to get it down on paper before it slipped from her.

After that, she steamed ahead and the book grew daily, till one fine day she realized that she had only two chapters to write.

"And I've done it myself," she murmured as she turned over the closely-written sheets. "Goodness knows I've *begun* piles in my time; but this is the first I've ever *finished*. Won't Madge be thrilled! I must get on with it, and then I can go over it, and correct, and so on. And then I can finish the typing. That oughtn't to take too long if I only stick in at it."

She glanced through it. It was not a really long book. Joey religiously counted the number of words on every sheet, and she knew that it would finish somewhere in the neighbourhood of forty thousand words. But it would be a *book*, even if it never found a publisher, and if she could write one, she could write another. Already her brain was teeming with ideas, but she had enough common sense to set them aside until her present work was done.

And then something happened which held her up appreciably—something of which she had never dreamed. All the same, her book did not suffer in the long run, though Joey was certain at first that it would. The chances are that *Cecily Holds the Fort* would never have been the book it was; might never have seen more of the light of day than what was in Joey's own room; it might never have been read by anyone but the two for whom it was intended, had it not been for that hindrance.

CHAPTER 6

The Problem of Polly

Contrary to the expectations of some people, Polly Heriot had soon settled down at school, and proved herself to be a law-abiding young person on the whole. After her years with an elderly governess, this coming amongst a horde of cheerful young people, who saw nothing wonderful in school but took life very much as it came, was a revelation.

Since her aunts' deaths, Polly had been able to satisfy *one* longing. Mr Wilmot had, as she truly said, been generous enough with her allowance, and Polly had indulged in an orgy of school stories. She had read at least fifty during the months before her illness; and when her guardian had asked during her convalescence what she wanted, she had begged for more. Mr Wilmot was only too anxious to do what he could, so he had sent an order to a famous firm to send down a dozen or so of their latest, and Polly had revelled in them.

Naturally, they had helped to colour her ideas of school, and when she found herself at the Chalet School, it was only her shyness that kept her from trying to find or fulfil all the adventures with which she had stuffed her mind. Fortunately the girls were usually too busy with their own concerns to trouble about imaginary adventures, though there *had* been a time – as Joey and her compeers could have told the new girl – when they had tried to copy as many of the customs of school stories as they could.

In the meantime, while Polly was settling down and

assimilating the ideas of the school as rapidly as she could, she was also presenting a problem to the staff.

"Polly Heriot is a bright child," declared Miss Wilson one evening when Polly had been there about a month. "But oh, my goodness! Her prior education leaves a good deal to be desired!" She surveyed the young lady's botany exercise with a rueful smile.

"What's wrong with it, Nell?" asked Miss Annersley, leaning across from her own table to examine it. "It looks neat enough."

"That's as may be. The trouble is that it's at least fifty years behind the times!" retorted Miss Wilson. "Just look at those *niggling* little sketches!"

"Oh, she's out of date," agreed the English mistress. "Her essays aren't essays at all – they're good little 'compositions', all nicely spelled, written, punctuated, and paragraphed, and without an original idea in them. Polly Heriot is an original young person when she isn't trying to express herself on paper."

"Her arithmetic is enough to turn anyone's hair white!" groaned Miss Leslie from the other side of the room. "Oh, beautifully neat, and set down with ruled lines and carefully formed figures. But I'd give a bookful of all this meticulous working for one untidy page of today's methods!"

"She's a problem!" commented Miss Wilson, as she scribbled a brief remark at the bottom of Polly's work and took up Joyce Linton's. "According to Kits, she doesn't even know how to do arithmetic. Her science is conspicuous by its absence; botany, mid-Victorian; geography, the limit – have I shown you the centipedes she draws for mountain ranges? – What's her history like, Con?"

"Oh, matches with the rest. Just what you'd expect

– fearfully biased stuff, and no idea of standing back and taking a good, general view of things," said Miss Stewart. "She knows all the dear old stories – Canute and the Waves, Alfred and the Cakes, and all the rest of it. As for anything outside of *English* history, Europe and the rest of the world might never have existed, so far as she's concerned!"

"Well, she's a problem," repeated Miss Wilson. "She's in Five B, but in most things she's scarcely fit for the Fourth. Jeanne!" She stretched out and poked Mademoiselle Lachenais in the back. "Wake up! Never mind that stuff you're reading! What have you to say about her French?"

"But, Nell!" expostulated jolly little Mademoiselle Lachenais as she regarded a blot of red ink the poke had caused her to drop on Gillian Linton's translation. "What, then, have I done?"

"Been deaf to the pearls of wisdom I'm pouring at your feet," said Miss Wilson. "Oh, never mind the ink! Mop it up – here's my blotchy! What I want to know is your opinion of Polly Heriot's French."

"Oh, but excellent!" exclaimed Mademoiselle. "She speaks prettily, and very fluently, and her knowledge of the grammar is good. She tells me that her aunts had a maid who was Parisienne, and they insisted that the child should converse with her every day. She must have been an educated woman, for Polly uses certain expressions that are quaint and old-fashioned, certainly, but always the purest of French."

"And Latin?" queried Miss Annersley, who was listening intently.

"That, also, is good. She can work with Five A, and – and 'keep her end up', as you say. She had special lessons

63

with Monsieur le Curé, whom she begged to teach her when she had lessons in her catechism from him."

"*Oh!*" groaned Miss Wilson. "What on earth are we to do with such anomaly?"

"I have an idea," said Miss Annersley.

With one accord, they turned and looked at her.

"What is it?" demanded Miss Wilson. "If you can solve this problem for us, Hilda, I shall immediately propose a vote of thanks to you."

Miss Annersley laughed. "What nonsense! All the same, don't you think it might be a good idea to turn Jo Bettany loose on her?"

"Not for maths, if you please!" said Miss Leslie decidedly. "Jo's ideas of maths are wild and woolly in the extreme."

"I wasn't thinking of maths," returned Miss Annersley. "But Jo could certainly coach Polly in history, which is her own subject; geography, in which you've always said she was good, Nell; and essay-writing. Apparently, the child's French and Latin can take care of themselves; but her German is enough to make one tear one's hair – so Sally Denny told me yesterday. Now Jo is good at languages, so she could give us a helping hand there. As for maths – where's Dorothy Edwards? – Dolly, could you give her a couple of periods a week?"

Miss Edwards shook her head. "Can't be done, my dear! I'm sorry, but I haven't a moment to call my own this term."

"Oh, I'll take her for maths if you like," said little Miss Nalder, the physical training mistress. "I used to be rather good at school. Kits, will you put me up to the latest dodges?"

"Like a shot! A couple of evenings will soon settle

that." Miss Leslie turned to Miss Wilson, laughing. "Nell, get up and propose that vote of thanks at once. The problem of educating – *what's* the child's hair-raising name? – Hildegard Mariana Sempronia – "

"Sophonisba," corrected Miss Annersley with a smile.

"What a name! Well, anyhow, the problem of how to get on with her education has been very neatly solved, it seems to me."

"Thank goodness for that!" ejaculated Miss Wilson. "Ladies, I rise to propose a vote of thanks to Miss Hilda Mary Annersley for being so clever. All agreed? Then please show in the usual manner.'

The staff broke into an outburst of applause, while Miss Annersley somewhat witheringly requested them not to be so silly. "You might be Middles!" she concluded.

The applause died down, and then Miss Leslie suggested that it would be well to send for Joey and break the news to her.

"I simply must see her face when you tell her the glad tidings!" she said. "How long is she likely to stay down? The twins must be nearly finished by this time; but haven't the other children begun?"

"Madame rang up this morning to say that, with the exception of poor little Peggy, *all* the invalids were doing very well," said Miss Annersley. "Peggy's had a bad dose, but she seems to be making progress now. Primula Mary is safe, thank goodness, and so are the babies. But Jo will have to stay here for at least another month, and she ought to have made quite an impression on Polly by that time."

"Another *month*! Why, that will bring it to past half term!" cried Miss Wilson. "Are you sure, Hilda?"

"Certain! Madame says she's taking no chances with Joey – *or* Primula Mary."

"No; that poor baby is still very frail, isn't she?" said Miss Wilson, looking serious. "That's the Queensland climate, I suppose?"

"Evidently. I've heard that North Queensland is worse than India."

"How is Mrs Venables managing at St Clare's?" asked Miss Edwards.

"Very well. She has the girls well in hand, and they like her. For one thing, she is tactful. For another, she never says anything she doesn't mean. And she *does* consult other and more experienced people and doesn't try to introduce new orders off her own bat," returned Miss Wilson.

"Oh, Mrs Venables has had a long family of her own. There were three little boys, besides Daisy and Primula," said Miss Annersley.

Dorothy Edwards raised her eyebrows. "Really? I'd no idea of that."

Miss Annersley nodded. "Yes; they died of the awful climate. Poor little soul; no wonder she clings to Daisy and Primula Mary."

"Well, this isn't sending for Jo and telling her what we want her to do," broke in Miss Wilson.

"But what about Jo's book?" asked Miss Leslie.

"Jo won't mind helping us," said Miss Annersley confidently. "And besides that, Matey doesn't want her to sit too closely at it. You know what Jo is when she does anything. Dorothy, do see if you can find a child somewhere, and send her to fetch Jo."

Dorothy Edwards got up, smiling. "All right. And I'm going straight back to St Agnes', or the good people there will be wondering if I've been kidnapped. Good night, everyone!" She took her departure, catching

66

Evadne Lannis in the corridor, and sending her to seek Jo and tell her she was wanted in the staff room.

"In the staff room? What on earth for?" demanded Jo when she heard the messenger.

"*I* don't know,' returned Evadne. "Teddy simply said to tell you they wanted you to go to them pronto."

"Oh, drat and drabbit it!" said Jo fervently. "I'd better go, I suppose. But I do wish people would leave me alone when I'm busy!"

"I guess you had, if you don't want the peach of a row," said Evadne, referring to the first part of her sentence.

Jo sighed and marched off, racking her brains on why she had received this unexpected summons.

She was welcomed by the staff, who offered her a chair and the box of sweets with which they had been regaling themselves. When she was comfortably settled, Miss Annersley unfolded the latest scheme to her, reducing her to breathlessness.

"Will you do it, Joey?" asked Miss Wilson.

"But – but – you surely don't mean you expect *me* to teach the kid?" gasped Jo, regardless of her language. "Why, she's only four years younger than me!"

"My dear girl, to Polly you are grown up – especially as your hair is – up, shall we say?" said Miss Annersley.

Joey clutched her head, and found that little tails were sticking out all round the funny little knobs she wore over her ears. "Oh, bother my hair! For two pins I'd have it cut off again tomorrow!" she vowed.

"Nonsense!" said Miss Annersley, coming to the rescue, and removing the pins to twist up the shaggy ends and repin them neatly. "Your hair grows very quickly, Jo, and it will be long enough to keep tidy by Christmas. Until then, try parting it into two tails and drawing them across each other at the back, and fastening them there. I think that might do it. Shall I come and show you at bedtime?"

"I wish you would," said Jo. "I'll be thankful for anything that will make me look less like a hedgehog!"

"But what about Polly?" asked Miss Leslie. "Will you take her on, Joey? They are your own subjects – we don't ask you to teach her maths – or drawing," she added with a twinkle, for a year before this Jo had had such a fuss with the short-tempered drawing master, Herr Laubach, that she had been removed from his classes.

Jo flushed at this reminder. "I couldn't teach maths if you paid me!" she retorted, leaving the question of drawing alone.

"We all know that," agreed Miss Wilson. "What we want to know is, will you take on Polly?"

"Oh, I'll do it if you really think I *can*. I'll do my best, anyhow."

"Of course you can do it," said Miss Stewart decidedly. "And Polly is a nice child, and won't try to play you up as some of those other young imps might."

"What exactly does it entail?" asked Jo.

"Well, lessons in European history, and a period for essay-writing," said Miss Annersley. "And Miss Wilson would be very grateful if you could give her one period in map-reading. And Miss Denny wouldn't be sorry if you gave her a couple of half-hours in German."

"All right," said Joey. "I'll take it on. My book is nearly finished, anyhow, and I've heard you should always let a book lie fallow for a week or two before you start correcting it. Anyhow, now that those wretched imps, David and Bride, have started measles, I might as well do

68

something for my board and lodging, seeing that I shall be down here for another month at least."

"And there's something more, Joey," added Miss Annersley. "If you are going to write school stories, you ought to have some idea of school life from *our* point of view. At present, you have next to none. We aren't always teaching or on our best behaviour, you know. If you can learn something about the staff side of a school, it will be all to the good."

Joey went beetroot-red at this public acknowledgment of her future work, but she knew that Miss Annersley was right, and that this was an exceptional opportunity for her to learn about a side of the school of which she knew very little. She murmured her thanks for the hint, and then, having settled with Miss Annersley, Miss Wilson, and Miss Stewart about the textbooks she should use, she said good night, and went back to her room and *Cecily*. She was gratified to find that the little break in the work had freshened her up and cleared her brain; and she was enabled to finish the last chapter but one before she went to bed that night.

CHAPTER 7

Joey Embarks on a New Career

It was not without some qualms that Joey picked up her *Histoire de l'Europe* at twenty-five minutes past eleven the next morning, and made her way downstairs to a small classroom that was generally used for private coaching. She would not have turned a hair if she had been asked to take on an entire form; but to face one girl, and have her all to herself for an hour and a half, required some doing. Besides, though no one would have believed it, and she would never have admitted it herself, Joey felt shy. She never minded meeting people, and her propensity for butting in on perfect strangers had brought her some queer experiences in her time. But this was entirely different.

Meanwhile, sitting with Five A who were reading *Voyage autour de mon Jardin*, Polly herself was feeling even worse. She had taken a great fancy to the tall, slim girl who had looked after her so competently that first day they had met. But since then Jo had spent each weekend at Innsbruck by special command of Matron; and during the week she had been too busy to be much at St Clare's. Moreover, Polly had heard all sorts of stories about her from her fellow Middles, who were tending to make a tradition of their late Head Girl.

The eleven-thirty bell rang, and while the rest of Five A streamed away to the science lecture room for a hard-working hour or so with Bill, Polly armed herself with history textbook, scribbler and pen, and made her way to the classroom, wondering what was going to happen.

Joey, seated at the mistress's table, looked up with a rather forced grin as her pupil entered. "Hullo, Polly! I thought you'd be coming along presently. Fetch yourself a chair, and come along and sit down."

Polly meekly laid down her books, brought the chair, and sat down on its extreme edge.

"I think," went on the new teacher, "that Miss Stewart said – Help! What *are* you doing?"

The floors of the Chalet School were kept well polished. Polly, balanced on the edge of her chair, standing on a floor like ice, slid away from it. She disappeared uncontrollably under the table, while the chair, under the impetus of her fall, shot to the other side of the room. Joey jumped up in some alarm, and hauled her to her feet, inquiring anxiously if she was hurt.

"No-o-o, thank you, I think not," said Polly, rather bewildered by the shock.

"But how on earth did you *do* it?" asked Jo.

"I – I don't know. It just – happened."

"Well, if you're sure you're not hurt – you *are* sure, aren't you? – bring that chair back, and we'll begin again."

Polly brought the chair, still rather mystified as to what had really happened, and this time sat on it firmly, determined that if it should go off again, it should take her with it.

"Miss Stewart says you've done no European history," began Joey again.

"No," said Polly shyly.

"Have you done any Greek or Roman history?"

71

"Yes; Mr Bryant, our curate, taught me lots when I went to him for Latin."

"Oh, good! Then I needn't waste any time over that. Suppose we begin with the Middle Ages? It's a very interesting period, all sorts of things happened then, and all sorts of famous people lived then. I suppose you've heard of Roland, and Charlemagne, and all those people?"

Polly nodded. "Yes; I've read about them. There were lots of books about them in the library at home, and I read all I could, until the aunts stopped me."

"Very well, then!" Jo spoke briskly. "We'll just start with France and the others at the beginning of the eleventh century. See here!" She produced an enormous sheet of cartridge paper which she spread out on the table showing Polly that it was divided into columns, each of which was headed with the name of a different country, with the exception of the first, which was for dates.

"What is it?" asked Polly curiously.

"It's a history chart – at least, it's *going* to be. I got Anne Seymour to do it for me. Look here; we put down a date *here* – 1000 to 1050, for example, and then we put down the different things that were happening in the different countries during that time, each in its proper column. See – here's the Holy Roman Empire. This is France. Here you have Spain. England's this column; and so on. It's awfully useful, for it does help you to keep things in their proper places. Then, if you like to put in pictures to illustrate any of the events, you can do so. Can you draw, by the way?"

"Herr Laubach doesn't think so," said Polly sadly. "He gets cross about everything I do."

Jo grinned. "I see. Well, do the best you can. And you can always cut out pictures – if they're small enough, of course – and paste them on so long as you do it neatly. D'you think you understand?"

"Yes, I think so. Anyhow, it looks very interesting," said Polly, whose earlier experience of history had included learning a chapter out of a very dull history book, and being questioned on it by Miss Smithson, who never permitted her pupil to do any of the questioning. This had been boring to Polly, who was full of curiosity about certain things. For instance, what would have happened if Wat Tyler had never been killed? Supposing the Roundheads had captured Charles II during his wanderings, would they have executed him as they did his father? Like most girls of her age and mentality, Polly was a Cavalier in feeling, and had shocked her prim governess by calling Oliver Cromwell "that horrid man".

Jo left her little time for thinking. Opening her history, she said, "Well, we'd better see what we can find to fill those columns; they look emptyish at present."

Polly opened her book too, and glanced rather helplessly at the first page. She really had no idea what to look for, though she was greatly thrilled at the prospect. Joey guessed it, and came to her help.

"Look here; the first event of the time is the death of the Emperor, Otto III. He died in 1002, and was succeeded by Henry II."

"But I thought Henry II's dates were 1154 to 1189," objected Polly.

"I mean the *Emperor* Henry II," explained Joey. "We aren't bothering with English history at the moment, though we must put in the events in their proper column, of course. Put your dates down in the right place, and then print in Otto's death."

Polly did as she was told, and then sat back, looking expectantly at Joey.

"France!" said that young lady. "Find the pages. Here you are!"

Polly glanced through the pages, and then turned eyes of dismay on her teacher. "There doesn't seem to be a thing," she said.

"Nothing fearfully exciting in the way of battles and so on. But this was the time of the Cluniac Reformation."

"What was that? I've never heard of it."

Jo sat back. "I suppose you've heard of St Benedict who founded the Benedictine Order of monks? Well, that happened a few centuries before this, and in the interval, the monks had fallen away from St Benedict's Rule. The Cluniac Reformation was begun at the Abbey of Cluny, to bring them back, and generally improve matters. Naturally, they got away rather from St Benedict's original idea, but they did a great deal of good, and tightened up things. That was important, for until the Renaissance brought in the Greek learning, and the printing press made books cheap, it was only the monks who kept alive any learning at all in the world. So it mattered very much that they should not be ignorant, nor idle, nor wicked. If they had been, goodness knows what would have happened, for the nobles couldn't even write their own names as a rule; and the secular clergy were generally too busy to spend the time copying old manuscripts and sending them round."

Polly pulled down her lips at the corners. "Oh?"

"Well, what did you expect?" demanded Jo reasonably. "If a priest had the care of a parish on his shoulders, he had about as much as he could do to look after it. But the monks were different. They lived in monasteries to sing God's praises in choir at regular hours of the day and

74

night; to pray for those who either couldn't or wouldn't pray for themselves. And as they had a certain amount of spare time on their hands after that, and St Benedict's Rule said that they must work as well as pray and praise, they spent a lot of their time in copying out the works of people like St Jerome, and – Irenaeus. Of course, some of them had to do field work; and others helped to build the glorious abbey churches. And then," went on the teacher, warming to her subject, "if anyone did want to learn, there were only the monasteries where he could go. And they were the doctors, too. And they looked after the poor, and orphans, for there weren't any workhouses in those days."

Polly sat with wide eyes. "Goodness! I'd no idea they did all that!" she exclaimed. "I thought they just sang and prayed and sat about meditating a lot, and enjoying themselves."

"Was it likely? Of course, just before the Cluniac Reformation, a number of the monasteries had fallen on evil days, and many of the monks were idle, I suppose. That was just why the Reformation started. But you don't suppose men were accepted into monasteries, and fed and clothed and generally looked after till they died, for nothing, do you?"

"Didn't they pay board or something?"

"I believe some of them brought money with them. But some of them were quite poor men. Now is it likely that they would be encouraged to sit down and do nothing?" demanded Jo.

"I – I suppose not," agreed Polly, who was assimilating some new and totally unexpected ideas.

"Well, then, use your common sense. And put down that Reformation. You can illustrate it by a picture of a Benedictine monk later on, if you like. I've got some somewhere."

Polly bent her head over the chart and printed in the words. The rest of the lesson passed quickly, and by the time Jo decreed that they had done enough history for one morning, Polly had something down in each column.

"You can read up about those events when you have time," said Jo. "And see what you can do about illustrations. It's a pity you can't draw – not that I can myself. But if you *could* have put in some jolly little original pictures, it would have made it much more interesting."

"Miss Smithson said I could sketch quite prettily," said Polly defensively. "It's only Herr Laubach who says I'm bad. He does get so worked up about my work."

Jo grinned reminiscently. "He can do that without even an excuse," she said feelingly. "But if you sketch 'prettily', my child, it's no wonder! 'Pretty' work is like a red rag to a bull with him."

"I don't see why," protested Polly.

"Well, he's all for the modern methods, you know. I've never seen your drawings, but I should imagine you put in piles of detail instead of taking 'a broad view', which is his mania – that, and seeing purple in every blessed thing. However, that's besides the point. In the meantime, we might try a little German for a change."

"I hate German," grumbled her pupil. "I don't see why we should have to learn such a sickening language."

"German is one of the chief languages in this school," was Jo's chill retort; "and I suppose you don't want to go dumb every third day here – for that's what will happen if you don't learn it. Besides, you don't suppose the staff would put up with that, do you? I can just see Bill's face if you refused to answer her because she was speaking to you in German!"

76

Polly gave it up after that. She had a very wholesome awe of Bill, and the thought of what her housemistress would be like if she had to deal with a suddenly-dumb pupil was more than enough to quell any ideas of rebellion on the part of the new girl. She listened quietly, which relieved her new governess. By the time the bell rang for the end of morning school, she had learned at least a little of the new language.

"You haven't done so badly for the first morning," said Joey. "You come to me at noon tomorrow. We'll tackle essay-writing, so you need only bring along your scribbler and a pencil, for that's all you'll require."

"Yes, Miss Bettany," said Polly.

"Jo, if you please," returned that young lady with a grin. "I'm not three months away – or, at least, not much more – from my own schooldays, and 'Miss Bettany' from people like you makes me feel nervous; so don't do it again. You'd better trot along now, or you'll be late for Mittagessen."

Polly, with a startled glance at her new wristwatch, fled on the word. She had not been at the Chalet School all this time without learning that punctuality was considered one of the most important of the minor virtues. Jo watched her out of sight, and then, habit swaying her, went off to the Sixth Form splashery to make herself presentable.

Margia Stevens and Elsie Carr were there for the same purpose, and they looked round as Jo entered.

"Hello, Joey!" said Margia. "What have you been doing with yourself all this morning?"

"Teaching," said Jo serenely. "Buck up with that soap, Elsie. I don't want to be late for Mittagessen, and there doesn't seem to be any more here."

Elsie tossed over the soap. "Teaching?" she said incredulously, ignoring Jo's last sentence. "Teaching what? Hadn't you better try a bigger bait while you are about it, my dear?"

"Oh, I'm not pulling your leg," said Joey, setting to work. "I really have been teaching."

"*Jo-seph-ine Bet-tany!*"

"Well, private coaching really," amended Joey. "I've had that new child, Polly Heriot, for history and German."

"Joey! What a priceless idea!" Elsie collapsed on a boot-locker in fits of laughter.

"What's there so priceless about it?" demanded Jo, slightly nettled. "Do you think I don't know enough?"

"No; you know enough to teach *us* in those two subjects, I should think. But it seems so weird for you to be *teaching* when it isn't so fearfully long since you were merely being *taught*," explained Elsie, rising from her uncomfortable seat on the lockers.

"What's the kid like to teach?" asked Margia, emerging from the towel with which she had been scrubbing her face dry. "Amy says she's the rummiest mixture in form. Some things she knows awfully well. Others she never even seems to have heard of. And I believe Bonny Leslie regularly has hysterics over her arithmetic, so it must be awful! Bonny's a calm sort of soul as a rule."

"She's bright enough," said Jo, rinsing her hands. "The trouble is that she seems to have been taught along the same lines as her own great-grandmother. Antiquated isn't the word for some of her ideas!"

"Anything like Stacie Benson when *she* first came?" demanded Elsie, pausing in the act of tying the ribbon that kept her bushy curls off her face.

78

"Oh, good gracious, no! Stacie wasn't antiquated – anything but! Polly is. However, she'll soon pick up different ideas, let's hope. Oh! There goes the gong! Come on or we shall be late!" And Jo dropped her towel, and led the race from the splasheries till she came to the common room, where she parted with the other two, remembering suddenly that she had been told at Frühstück that for the future her place would be with the staff.

"I suppose I should have used the staff splashery, too," she thought as she made her way rather more decorously to the staff room. "What a horrid bore! Still, I'd better remember, or Mademoiselle will have things to say."

At Mittagessen, those of the staff sitting near her asked, with some curiosity, how she had got on.

"Oh, all right, I think," said Jo casually.

"I'm thinking of asking you to take two or three other girls for German coaching, Joey," said Miss Denny, who was responsible for all modern languages but French. "Joyce Linton is still appallingly shaky over grammar, though she can chatter well enough on occasion. And Mary Shaw and Enid Sothern could do with extra work, too. Will you take them on?"

"But they couldn't work with Polly," objected Jo. "She knows next to nothing about it, and is just at the 'have-you-the-book-of-my-father?' stage."

"I know that. But you could take them another time. There are three afternoons in the week when they don't have games, and if you could take them for an hour or so then, it would help both them and me enormously."

Jo looked blue; but Mademoiselle Lepâttre nodded encouragingly at her. "Why not, ma petite? You could do it, and you would find the work very interesting, I assure you."

"It wasn't exactly my idea of life," murmured Jo.

"All the same, Joey, those three more hours a week wouldn't hurt you," put in Miss Annersley in her gentle voice. "As Miss Denny says, it would do those children a world of good."

"Anyway, I shan't be here more than a month or so," Jo pointed out.

"Even so, that would do quite an amount for those three," said Miss Denny cheerfully. "Miss Norman can't take on any extra coaching this term, she has so many new children at St Agnes', and her time is fully occupied. And I have piano lessons every afternoon, or I would take them myself."

"Jo will consider the matter and discuss it with me – eh, Joey?" said Mademoiselle. "We will have Kaffee und Kuchen together this afternoon, in the study, my Jo, and talk about it then."

Whatever happened during that talk, Mademoiselle won the day for Miss Denny, and when Jo rang up the Sonnalpe next morning, it was to inform her startled sister that she had agreed to take over the other three for German.

"It's only for two or three weeks, anyhow," she said cheerfully.

"That's all you know!" came back Mrs Russell's voice, accompanied by a half-rueful laugh.

"Madge Russell, what do you mean?"

"Only that Rix has a cough which Jem says sounds uncommonly like whooping cough. He's not sure yet, and we're keeping Master Rix in strict quarantine. But he certainly has a distinct tendency to whoop, and if that's the case, you're likely to have to stay down much longer than either of us bargained for, my child."

"But how on earth has he managed to get whooping cough when he's been in quarantine for measles?"

"That's what *we* wanted to know. It seems that Master Rix has struck up a friendship with another small boy whose people are out here – and the pair have been hob-nobbing over the palings for the last three days, if not more."

"But what was he doing out?"

"Oh, well, he's never been really ill, and the weather has been so lovely – what's taken you, Jo? Why are you mooing at me like that?"

"Only the weather," said Jo with another unearthly groan. "It's been pouring cats and dogs here!"

"Poor you! It's been glorious here. I did notice that the clouds were down, but I didn't bother about it. We've had wonderful sunshine – a real Indian summer. Rix being really quite well in himself, he's been wrapped up and allowed to be in the garden for a couple of hours every day lately, so he met Alan Lindsay – probably exchanged illnesses with him too. Jack Maynard was attending Alan for whooping cough, and as far as we can gather, the pair of them have been breathing heavily on each other during the past few days. They're both safely penned up again now, and fortunately they're the sturdiest little pair of ruffians you could find anywhere."

"And the others?"

"Oh, never near it. Peggy's been too weak for visitors, and the other invalids are still strictly quarantined. But this means that you and the Robin and Primula Mary and Stacie can't come near us for weeks to come."

"Well, I could just shake young Rix for this! Bother him! Why must he go chumming up with a whooping kid at this stage of the proceedings?"

"Mischief, I suppose," said Rix's aunt cheerfully. "Joey, I must ring off now. Call you tomorrow."

"All right! Goodbye! Give my love to everyone!" Joey hung up the receiver, and turned to Mademoiselle who had just come in, and knew all about it.

"I should like to box Rix's ears!" she wailed. "Madge won't let me go near the Sonnalpe till this is over, I know. Whooping cough was one of the things I *did* manage to miss when I was small, and I know she won't take the smallest risk of it now."

"I do not blame her for that. Whooping cough is so much worse when one is grown up. Now I must go to see Matron before Prayers. And you?"

"Oh, I shall go and write the last chapter – or as much of it as I can manage before twelve o'clock. Then I'll put the thing away for a few days before I correct it. If this wretched weather would only clear, we might get some hockey."

"Perhaps it will," said Mademoiselle soothingly. "You have done well to finish your book so soon, chérie. I shall look forward to reading it."

Jo laughed. "It's not a very big book. But it's the first I've ever accomplished, so that's something." Then she went off to wind up the tale of Cecily's exploits, which she managed to do just before the school clock chimed twelve.

CHAPTER 8

Polly Creates a Sensation

Polly Heriot was enjoying school. After the dull years in a schoolroom all to herself, with only an elderly governess for companion, she found lessons in company with eighteen or twenty other girls and a succession of mistresses quite a thrill. The work she did by herself with Jo was another joy, for Jo, whatever her shortcomings as a teacher, did not include dullness among them. All things considered, therefore, Polly was having a good time.

Apart from lessons, there were games – when the weather permitted – and the various out-of-school ploys with which the Chalet girls occupied themselves, a quite important one being the Hobbies Club, where they met together once a week to compare notes and pursue various handicrafts. Joey cut jigsaws with a treadle-machine. Elsie Carr had taken up painting on china. Gillian Linton went in for leatherwork, and her younger sister, Joyce, showed a decided gift for chip-carving. For two hours on one night in the week, the girls used the big common room for their collections and crafts, the one stipulation being that they should clear up the mess before they went to bed.

Polly had no hobby. The only handcraft her great-aunts had approved was sewing. Let loose among all sorts of interesting things, she had no idea what to choose, though everyone was generous with suggestions and advice. Many of them offered to start her in any collection she liked to choose; but Polly was a canny young person, and she decided to wait a little before deciding. Meanwhile, after a survey of the various handcrafts, she made up her mind to go in for painting on wood. In spite of Herr Laubach's judgment, she was really quite artistic, and once she had realized that the delicate, finicking brushwork adored of Miss Smithson was no use here, she did very well. She began with small boxes and trays of white wood, and took a keen delight in the unnatural-looking posies with which she adorned them. By the time she had provided three pretty boxes of various kinds, all beautifully decorated, she had a wild craze for her work, and her one grief was that Hobbies Club couldn't be held every night.

One evening, about a week after Rix Bettany's latest outbreak, Polly came down to the common room, armed with paints, brushes, and a hand mirror which she proposed to paint as a Christmas gift for Miss Wilmot.

"What will you put on it?" asked Joey.

"Daisies and buttercups," said Polly promptly. "I got the design out of that book that Herr Laubach keeps in the art cupboard."

"Which book is that?" demanded Gillian Linton, who had overheard the conversation.

"I forget the name of it. Anyway, it's German, and I'm not sure that I could pronounce it, even if I remembered it. But it's about designs and how to use them. I've got it in my desk in Five B. I'm just going to fetch it. There are hundreds of designs, I should think, and this one is so pretty, and very simple. See; I've drawn it already!" And she exhibited the back of the mirror to show the simple, pretty wreath she had drawn there.

"You'd better put Miss Wilmot's initials in the centre," suggested Jo. "Hasn't Herr Laubach got a book on lettering somewhere? Ask him; I feel sure he has. But, I say! you *must* be improving in your drawing!"

"He hasn't ragged me the last two lessons," admitted Polly, as she laid down the mirror, and ran off to get the book.

When she came back, somewhat breathless – for it was a veritable tome – the others were all busy with their own work, even Jo being fathoms deep in an extra large jigsaw. Polly laid the book on the table she was using, found her place, and settled down happily with paints and brushes to reproduce the colouring.

Jo chanced to look up presently, and her eyes widened as she saw what the book was. "Polly Heriot! You don't mean to say that Herr Laubach has lent you *that*!" she exclaimed.

Polly flushed slightly. "Not exactly," she said.

Jo got up and came over to her. "How do you mean – 'not exactly'?"

"Well, it was on the shelf, and I thought we could borrow anything from there, so I took it. Isn't it all right?" asked Polly in some alarm.

"Of course it isn't! It's all wrong! Do you really suppose that Herr Laubach intended all and sundry to borrow a book like that? Why, it must be a really valuable affair with those coloured plates. Take it back, Polly, before any harm comes to it. And don't borrow from those shelves again without permission. Otherwise, Herr Laubach may have something to say."

Polly got up reluctantly, and closed the book. Then she suddenly opened it again. "I must just see how the colours go for my mirror!" she pleaded.

Jo removed her painting water, and then said, "Now trot off with it. You've looked at it quite long enough."

Polly went off reluctantly, still gazing earnestly at the plate which showed her design. Jo, engaged in putting back the painting water, never saw her.

"If I had," she said later, "I'd have told the little ass to shut the book up. Then it might never have happened."

As it was, however, she said nothing about it, and the woeful result was that, never heeding where she was going, Polly tripped over a mat in the corridor, and fell headlong, the book beneath her. She was not hurt, but the book *was*. Polly was a well-grown person for fourteen, and beneath her weight, several pages, including the precious illustration at which she had been looking, were badly crumpled.

Too horrified to cry out, she stood with the book in her hands, looking at it with eyes that seemed ready to fall out of her head. What to say or do, she did not know. She only knew that there was going to be trouble for her – and bad trouble, too.

She was still wondering what she should do, when there came the sound of quick, light steps behind her, and then a voice said, "Why Polly! Why are you blocking up the corridor like this?"

She turned to meet the sapphire-blue eyes of Gillian Linton; and something in them caused her to hold out the book as well as she could, half-sobbing, "Look – look what I've done!"

Gillian snatched the volume from her hands – nearly dropping it, incidentally, for it was exceedingly heavy – and surveyed the damage with horrified face.

"Polly! What in the world were you going to do with this?"

"I took it to get the design," said Polly with a gasp. "I

– I didn't know. Oh, Gillian, will Herr Laubach be very cross with me?"

"Cross? He'll be raving!" ejaculated Gillian. "Why, he scarcely lets *me* look at it when he's there to turn over the pages. Oh Polly, what possessed you to do such a thing?"

"I thought we could always take those books on the shelf. And I never meant to fall. Oh, Gillian! Whatever will he do?"

Gillian looked at the crumpled pages again. They were badly bent, and Herr Laubach would certainly be furious. At the best of times he was peppery; so what he would be like over such an accident as this, Gillian could not imagine.

And then, the very worst thing that could have happened – or so it seemed to the two girls – burst on them. A door further along the corridor opened, and Herr Laubach himself appeared! He had stayed up at Briesau in order to make some arrangements with Mademoiselle about classes, and was just going off to the Adalbert Hotel, where he was to spend the night. Naturally, seeing the two girls standing there, horror in both their faces and attitudes, he came to inquire what was wrong. Equally naturally, he took it all in at a glance, and only consideration for the wan-looking lady he had just left kept him from a vociferous outburst of wrath then and there.

He looked round, and his suppressed anger was dreadfully apparent to the terrified Polly, who tried to get behind Gillian and make herself as small as possible. Then he swung across the hall, opened a door and motioned the pair into the room, where he switched on the lights. It was that same room in which Polly had her extra coaching with Joey, and it seemed to her that though on those occasions it was a very pleasant, bright little place, now it was heavy with gloom.

Herr Laubach followed them in, and shut the door behind him. Then he faced them. "Now," he said in his own language, his voice shaking with fury, "I will know what all this means?" He pointed to the tome which Gillian still held.

Polly took a step forward. "It – it wasn't Gillian," she said shakily. "It was me."

But Gillian interfered. "Herr Laubach," she said, speaking German, "Polly is new, and she thought she might borrow books from the shelves. She took this one to copy *this* design." She held it out that he might see. "She was taking it back, and tripped, and fell with the book. But I know she is very sorry, and wishes to beg your pardon."

"Now if there *was* a girl in this school who should not have dared such an impudence to commit, I should have chosen this one," returned Herr Laubach, pointing to the shrinking Polly. "But to take without leave my so-precious book! To fall down with it and crush the pages like this!"

Understanding only that he was angry, Polly was unable to say anything; but Gillian was quick to defend her. She said afterwards that Polly's need must have given her own German a good "shove-on", for she had had no idea she could be so fluent.

"Polly doesn't understand German yet, I'm afraid, Herr Laubach," Gillian said apologetically. "But she really is sorry, and if there is anything she can do to repair the damage she has done, she will do it."

All this time, she had been holding the damaged book. Now the drawing master took it from her, and going to the mistress's table, laid it down, and examined the injuries carefully. With his long, sensitive fingers, he smoothed out the crumpled pages, but they didn't look very much better. His eyes gleamed with anger as he saw them. He swung round on Polly, who nearly shrank back again.

"See what you have done!" he growled. "I much desire you to punish! Naughty child! Why have you my so-beautiful book take and him destroyed."

"I – I'm sorry," faltered Polly, "but I was looking at it one day, and I saw that lovely wreath, and – and it w-was just what I w-wanted for my m-mirror, and I didn't know I-I m-mustn't."

He glanced from her to the coloured plate, his heavy brows knitted. "You say you have this wreath copied? And for a mirror? Go; bring me your mirror, that I may for myself see if you the truth have spoken."

"I never tell lies!" said Polly haughtily, her fear suddenly going at this insult.

"So! Well, we will see. Go and the mirror her bring."

Polly stalked off, her cheeks burning at the thought that she was being disbelieved. She entered the common room furiously and Joey looked up. "Hello! What an age you've been? Get it safely put away?"

"No! That pig of a Herr Laubach caught Gillian and me after I'd fallen down with it, and he's sent me for the mirror because he doesn't believe I'm drawing the wreath!" Polly seized her mirror, and was off again before Joey could pull her up for her unparliamentary language.

Straight into the little classroom she burst, and thrust her work at Herr Laubach, crying, "Here it is! And Gillian can tell you that it is all my own work!"

He grunted, and took the thing. He examined the carefully drawn wreath, at first in silence; then with an exclamation. Polly had just begun to tint the daisies when

Joey had interfered, so there was not much done. But what she had painted was done with a steady, self-assured stroke, and showed nothing of the stippling he had so girded at in her class sketches.

"You have this yourself getan?" he grunted at length.

"Certainly!" Polly's head couldn't go any higher, but her grey eyes were flashing.

"Then why have you such shocking work to me shown? You can like this paint, and you the most terrible vork me show. Why, I ask?"

Polly was gravelled. She had no idea what he meant. To tell the truth, she only understood half of what he was saying, for his broken English and queer accent were almost beyond her. Moreover, as he became more excited, he also became more incoherent, so she could only say, "Yes," and hope she was saying it at the right places.

Herr Laubach poured questions on her, and finally Gillian had to take a hand. In the course of the talk, she explained to him about the Hobbies Club, and he promptly demanded to be taken to it. With his book tucked under one arm, and the mirror in his other hand, he marched the girls off to the common room, where the little company certainly created a sensation when they arrived. Elsie Carr started so violently that she made a bad smear of violet beside the pansies she was painting on a tall jar. Joey stopped her machine so suddenly that she snapped her saw-blade. Anne Seymour pulled at her leather so violently that she puckered it; and Jeanne le Cadoulec got her lace bobbins twisted, and evolved a new and original quirk in her lace pattern.

The master looked round at them. "And so this is how you young ladies occupy your spare time?" he remarked. "Ah, Fräulein Joey. What do you do?"

"Jigsaw puzzles," said Jo briefly, for she was too much startled to think of anything else to say.

He came and examined her machine; questioned her about it, insisted on seeing how she worked; and then he amazed her by asking if she took orders.

"No," said Jo, still amazed into curtness.

"But I request that you will take mine, at least," he said. "Will you make for me two puzzles? And accept money at the usual cost?"

"I can't take money for a hobby," said Joey. "I'll cut the puzzles if you like."

He glanced at her. "You could use it to buy other materials for your work which, I know, you make for your bazaar," he remarked. "But if you are too proud to accept money for an order, I am too proud to accept as a gift that which I *ordered* as a customer."

"Oh," said Jo slowly.

"And I wish those puzzles," he continued. "See, mein Fräulein, I have a sick wife who must always lie on her couch. She finds the day long and dreary, and this would be a new entertainment for her."

"But if you'd let me, I'd love to cut puzzles for her," said Jo, pulling herself together.

"Another time, perhaps. But this time, I have asked it of you."

Jo was silent. The idea of using her hobby otherwise than to give pleasure had never dawned on her before. But she could see the drawing master's point. What is more, she saw something in his eyes that she had never seen before. She finally gave in. "I shall be very pleased to do as you ask me, Herr Laubach. But you must allow me to add another for Frau Laubach as – as a love-gift."

He nodded, and turned abruptly away to ask Elsie Carr

91

what she was doing, to find fault with some details of her work, and to push her unceremoniously from her seat, and show her what he meant. Then he passed on to Jeanne le Cadoulec, and from her to someone else, till he had gone all the rounds. Finally, he came back to the mirror. He sat down in Polly's chair, painted a buttercup and daisy for her, giving her rapid instructions all the time, and finally rose.

"When you wish to borrow my books," he said, speaking very slowly that she might understand, "please come and ask. And, young ladies," he turned to the others, "this is an excellent thing. If my knowledge can give you any assistance, please ask for it. Now I will wish you Gut' Abend, and go to my hotel." He bowed to them, and then departed, leaving them all gasping with the shock.

Once he had gone, Gillian danced a Highland fling in a corner of the room. "That's Polly you've got to thank for that!" she said, when she had finished. "I'd no idea he could be such an old duck!"

Jo was silent. She was recalling the look in the drawing-master's eyes when he had spoken of his invalid wife. "I'll give him that puzzle I've got upstairs tomorrow," she decided. "He can't leave before it's light, and I doubt if he will before Frühstück. I can run round to the hotel with it, and ask them to give it to him. Poor soul! It must be ghastly to have to be away from her most of the week, and know that she's dull and bored most of the time."

Herr Laubach kept his word, and thereafter took a deep interest in the Hobbies Club. So it was felt that, although Polly had certainly had no right to help herself to his book, still it hadn't turned out badly; so she heard no more of it from anyone. All the same, as Evadne truly remarked, she had succeeded in creating a fine sensation that night, for no one had ever suspected that Herr Laubach could take an interest in anything apart from his classes.

Perhaps the one who most benefited of all was poor, dreary Frau Laubach, who found her days becoming unexpectedly brighter when she had puzzles to occupy her. Joey also made opportunities to call and see her whenever she was in Innsbruck, and further insisted that Frieda Mensch should also go at least once a week. The new interests cheered her so considerably that she became quite a different woman. Jeanne le Cadoulec, brought down by Joey, showed her how to make simple stitches in pillow-lace, till finally she was able to weave great lengths of pretty lace, which found a ready sale. Then Frau Laubach's joy was complete. Altogether, Polly's sensation proved to be quite a success.

CHAPTER 9

The Result of Too Many School Stories

"Evvy, what is that bell up there for?"

Evadne Lannis turned round from Cornelia and Elsie, with whom she was strolling round the playing fields, to look up at the little tower which crowned Ste Thérèse's, and held a large bell swung by a rope.

"Oh, that's the Ste Thérèse bell," she said casually.

"Yes; but when is it rung? I mean, it doesn't call us to lessons or anything like that," persisted Polly, who was the questioner. "What use is it?"

"It's the alarm bell," said Elsie Carr, joining in the discussion. "If there should be a flood or a fire, that bell's rung, and we have to get to safety as quickly as we can."

"A flood!" gasped Polly. "Do you mean that the lake sometimes overflows?"

"Nonsense!" said Evadne. "Of course it doesn't!"

"It can soak the path with its waves, though, in a gale," Elsie reminded her. "It did last spring, you remember."

Evadne grinned. "Yes; that's so. But it never rises above its shores, and that, I guess, is what Polly meant."

"Well, I did," agreed Polly. "But if the lake doesn't overflow, what makes the floods?"

Elsie waved a dramatic hand towards the place where the mountain stream flowed into the lake from the great Tiernjoch which overshadowed the whole valley. "*That* does! We've had one flood since I came here; and there was one before. You'll have to get Evvy to tell you about that, though, for I hadn't come then."

"Really, Evvy?" Polly sounded excited. "Do tell me about it!"

"Not much to tell," said Evadne. "It was our first spring here, and happened during the thaws. The stream got choked higher up, and when the barrier gave, the water simply came down like – like a wall. We'd all gone to bed, and the first thing we knew, it was swooshing all round like mad. Wasn't there a mess when it went down, though!"

"What did they do?" asked Polly eagerly. "What a gorgeous adventure! I wish something like that would happen this term!"

"Something like what?" demanded a fresh voice, as Jo Bettany, accompanied by two or three of the Seniors, sauntered up to them. "What are you people talking about?"

"The flood we had that first spring we were here," explained Evadne.

Jo laughed. "Wasn't it a thrill! D'you remember how Madame and the staff got the wind up early in the day, and we had to clear all the lower rooms?"

"Rather!" said Margia Stevens. "I say. Jo! D'you remember Plato and Sally were with us, and how Plato hauled us all out on to the stairs and made us sing when the worst was past?"

"I do! And we had hot cocoa and biscuits in our dormies before that."

"And the next two days, when the waters had gone down, we had lessons up there, too," added Paula von Rothenfels.

"True for you. The Seniors helped to clear up, but we were out of all the fun!" sighed Jo.

"And the next year, there was that awful thunderstorm in the summer term when the thunderbolt fell in the field, and we were all pushed out in doublequick time, because everything was so dry, and the grass had caught fire," added Evvy. "Wasn't it fearful when the hail came, though? I was right away from the house, and by the time I got back, I was all bruises."

"What gorgeous fun!" sighed Polly. "Do you think such a thing is likely to happen again?"

"Oh, you never can tell," said Jo airily. "We're not likely to have such a fearful flood again, for they deepened the bed of the stream in the summer, and built up the banks with concrete – as you can see for yourself."

"And anyway, there's the big ditch to drain off the water all round us. That's why it was dug," added Cornelia.

"Oh, I *wish* it hadn't!" cried the sensation-seeking Polly. "I'd just love to be in a flood!"

"I guess that would depend on where you were while it was going on," retorted Cornelia, with a thought for her friend, Stacie Benson, who, nearly two years before, had been caught in a cleft in the mountains by another, though lesser, torrent, and who had paid for it by injuring her spine so that this was only her second term at the school. Cornelia thought that even Polly wouldn't care to be in a flood like that.

"You don't know what you're talking about," said Jo. "A flood's a pretty ghastly thing, my child. Hello! There's the bell for the end of break. We must adjourn this happy meeting."

She turned, and led the way to the school, the others following; and in the usual turmoil of lessons, books and all their other ploys, no one gave another thought to the conversation – except Polly herself. She was wild with envy of those who had experienced the two adventures mentioned, and only wished that a similar affair might fall to her lot.

"It wouldn't be so bad if the alarm bell was rung for a false alarm," she thought as she promenaded by the side of her partner, Klara Melnarti, when they took their daily walk round the lake. "What a joke it would be to ring it and have everyone out of bed in the middle of the night! Just like the school stories, too! I wonder – "

However, at this moment, Klara claimed her attention, and her thinking had to end for the time being. Only for the time being, however. Once she had got the idea, Polly brooded over it, wondering and wondering how she could manage to carry it out. It would be very difficult to do it at night, for she was over at St Clare's, and, try how she would, she could *not* see how she was to get downstairs, through the covered-in passage, and up to the top landing of Ste Thérèse's, without waking someone during her travels.

Most girls would have given it up; but Polly, coming late to school, and with most of her ideas based on the stories with which she had crammed her brain during the past year or so, had no mind to give it up. What is more, she determined to keep it to herself – which was a pity, for if she had taken any of her friends into her confidence, they would have given her some information which would have effectually stopped her. But many of Polly's books had described how the new girl came to the school, and, either by an act of heroism, or by saving the school at games, or else by her mischievous pranks, became the leader of the school. Polly had enough sense to know that acts of heroism don't turn up for the asking. Games were out of the question at present, for the heavy rains had turned the playing fields – both at the Chalet and at its friendly rival's St Scholastika's – into a morass. There remained, therefore, the mischievous prank idea.

It seemed to Polly that if she could ring that bell, and bring them all out, they would be so thrilled by the daring of the act that she would become a real live school heroine. "Just like in *Pat, the Pride of the School*," she thought, with a recollection of the heroine of one of her favourite tales.

Polly then turned her attention once more to the problem of how to get from St Clare's to Ste Thérèse's in order to ring the bell. She was so absorbed that she never noticed that Anne Seymour, who was taking preparation for the Middles, cast more than one glance at her, and therefore she jumped violently when her name was called.

"Polly Heriot! Have you finished your prep?"

"Er – no-o," stammered Polly, with a sudden remembrance of French, geography, and arithmetic not touched.

"Then do you mind getting on and not dreaming?"

"Yes, Anne," murmured Polly. She looked at the problem she had been trying to work out according to Miss Leslie's directions, and heaved a deep sigh. It is very difficult to have to turn round and work all your sums by quite new rules when the old ones are always tugging at your memory.

She struggled with it sadly, and finally set her exercise book aside, thankful that she had got some sort of answer to every one of the five sums. French was easy to her, but geography was not; and with the knowledge of Anne's sarcastic tongue, she dared not waste any more time.

And then fate suddenly came to her aid. Breaking through the quiet of the preparation room, came the sound of a dull *Thud!* followed by several lesser ones. The girls looked up eagerly, glad of an excuse to do so. Even Anne stopped for a moment in her task of explaining to Biddy O'Ryan the mysteries of highest common factors and raised her head with a startled air.

"Anne, what do you think that was?" asked Joyce Linton.

"Something fallen down – perhaps one of the pictures next door," said Anne. "It can't be anything very much. Go on with your work, all of you. Biddy, pay attention to me!"

Nothing more was said. The Middles obediently returned to their work, and Biddy, with a backward fling to one of the long pigtails that kept falling over her shoulders, fixed her attention once more on the troublesome arithmetic.

Twenty minutes later, the door opened, and St Clare's matron entered. The girls rose to their feet, but Mrs Venables nodded to them to sit down again and go on with their work before she called to Anne to come with her, saying that Miss Wilson wished to speak to her. Anne sent Biddy back to her seat, with strict injunctions to use her brains and be careful, and then followed the tiny lady from the room.

Five minutes later, Alixe von Elsen, one of the wilder spirits among the Middles, returned from her practising, and there was that in her face as she entered which made every girl sit up, while a subdued chorus demanded to know what had happened.

"The ceiling of the Wheatfield Dormitory has fallen down, and the beds are all in a most terrible mess, and no one can sleep there tonight," announced Alixe with satisfaction.

"The ceiling fallen down? But however could it do that?" cried Joyce Linton.

"No one knows. But I heard Bill say that it was the last done, and the men had been obliged to hurry with it, and it was – was – scamped work, I think she said. At least it is down, and everything is white with plaster. No one knows what to do with those who sleep there, for none of the beds in the upstairs dormitories is aired or made up, and there is not time tonight. Also, Kitty Burnett is in the san with influenza, and Nurse says that no one is to be with her," explained Alixe.

"P'raps they'll let us share beds for once," suggested Mary Shand, who was an inmate of Wheatfield Dormitory.

"Talk sense!" retorted Joyce crushingly. "You know as well as I do that our beds wouldn't hold us comfortably. Those that shared would have to spend the night clinging to the bed like grim death."

"It's much more likely they send us over to Ste Thérèse's," said Stacie, as she leaned back in her invalid chair with a sigh. "Some of the Seniors are away for the weekend, so their beds will be vacant. Elsie and Evvy have gone up to the Sonnalpe to stay with Elsie's people, I know. And some of the others went down to Innsbruck because they have to go to the dentist's, and Mademoiselle thought they'd better go this afternoon and stay overnight, now the trains have stopped running."

"*Girls!* Is this how you behave when you are left alone for a few minutes?" Miss Stewart came into the room and surveyed them all. "You ought to be ashamed of yourselves! Sit down at once, and go on with your work. The following girls will put their books away, and come with me: Stacie Benson – Polly Heriot – Suzanne Mercier – Alixe von Elsen – Biddy O'Ryan – Klara Melnarti. Be quick, you six, and don't waste any time." She left the room, and shut the door behind her.

"Coo!" murmured Joyce. "What's gone wrong with Charlie?" Then she buried her head in her books, for the door opened again as Miss Stewart looked in to say, "Bring your attaché cases with you if they are down here."

Stacie got up wearily, for her back had been aching off and on all day. Though she was practically well, there was a weakness which would last during all her growing years, and now and then she had these attacks of dull pain which reminded her that, though she was permitted to be in school again, she must take no liberties.

Suzanne noticed her fatigue. "But go on, Stacie chérie. I will bring your case and put away your books," she said gently.

"Will you, Suzanne? Thank you so much. My back really has been a nuisance today," said Stacie gratefully. She left the room slowly, and while the others shuffled their books together, Suzanne dealt quickly and efficiently with her friend's as well as her own. Then she hurried off after the rest, to find Matron, Miss Wilson, and Miss Nalder all busy in the Wheatfield Dormitory, while its ordinary occupants waited by the door with their cases.

"Here are your things, Stacie," said Miss Wilson, bringing them out. "Put them into your case, and then trot off to Ste Thérèse's. Wait a moment," she added, as her eye was caught by the flush in the girl's cheeks and the black shadows beneath her eyes. "Has your back been troubling you?"

"Just a little," said Stacie truthfully.

"Then leave your case here, and go straight to Matron. – Polly, you can take Stacie's things with your own. Go to

Matron's room when you have packed, and she'll tell you where to put them."

"Yes, Miss Wilson," said Polly in subdued tones. She dared speak in no other, for inwardly she was seething with excitement. Never had she imagined that things would go so well for her plan! It must come off tonight, of course, for she guessed that those in authority would see to it that one of the unused dormitories at the top of St Clare's would be made ready for them next day.

Miss Wilson got Polly's things together, and brought them to her. "There you are! Pack as quickly as you can, and get off. Whatever else you want, you must get tomorrow after Frühstück. You have everything you'll need for the night."

Polly quickly packed her possessions, caught up Stacie's case, and set off to Ste Thérèse's, and upstairs again to Matron's room, where she found that lady busy settling Stacie on a narrow sofa, a pillow under the aching shoulders and a light rug thrown over her.

"You should have told Matron Venables your back was troubling you," she was saying, as Polly came in. "I'm afraid this means spending tomorrow lying flat, Stacie. You are a silly girl, you know. Well, Polly?"

"Please, Matron, this is Stacie's case. Miss Wilson told me to bring it to you," said Polly meekly.

"Oh, very well. Set it down in the corner there, and then you can go upstairs to the Green Dormitory, where you are to sleep. Gillian Linton is there to show you your cubicle. Now run along, for I've so much on my hands, I don't know where to begin."

Polly nodded to Stacie, and departed to find Gillian Linton in the dormitory. Gillian welcomed her, showed her which cubicle she was to occupy, helped her to unpack her case, and then suggested that Polly should find her way downstairs to the common room.

"The gong will sound for Abendessen soon," she said. "It must be nearly nineteen hours, now. You go down, and the rest will come along presently."

Polly went downstairs, thrilling with the knowledge that she had been given the cubicle nearest the door. It should be easy for her to slip out, give the bell rope a few good hard tugs, and get back without being discovered. She calculated that in the first excitement of being wakened so unexpectedly, no one would notice whether she were there at the beginning or not. That her plan was likely to upset a good many people, among them Stacie (who was certainly not fit for such a shock), never occurred to her.

For the rest of the evening she was very quiet – so much so, that Jo, thinking there must be something wrong, came over and sat down to chatter to her till bedtime, which came at the usual early hour for the six Middles who were visiting.

Polly had very little to say, and Jo finally tired of trying to carry on a one-sided conversation, and went off to dance with Gillian, who was feeling rather worried about her unexpected responsibility. Four of the St Clare folk were billeted in the Green Dormitory, the other two being in the Yellow, so Gillian would certainly have to keep her eyes open, for among her four were included Alixe von Elsen, one of the naughtiest girls that ever wore the Chalet School uniform, though to look at she was a little saint; and Stacie, who had gone to bed, tired out with the pain in her back.

For once, Polly had nothing to say when bedtime came. She hurried upstairs with the rest, and undressed in silence. They had been warned to make as little noise as possible, as Matron hoped Stacie would sleep soon and wake better in the morning. But Stacie herself was very wide awake when they reached the dormitory, and only too anxious to talk to take her mind off her own discomfort.

"How silent you are, Polly," said Suzanne Mercier, as she stood in the middle of the room, brushing out her long, thick hair. "Are you, then, not well?"

"I am quite well, thank you," said Polly politely. "Only, I'm thinking."

"It must be something very heavy!" said Stacie, with a forlorn attempt at a laugh. "You might tell us, Polly."

"I beg your pardon, but it is private – at present," said Polly.

"Oh – sorry! I couldn't know, of course," apologized Stacie.

"It's all right," said Polly. She laid down her hairbrush, and presented herself to Suzanne to have her thick hair plaited for the night. Under her great-aunts' régime a maid had always attended to her flowing locks, and even now, if left to herself, she was apt to get it fearfully tangled. Suzanne was good-natured, and had undertaken to help with her mane of hair. She plaited it into two loose pigtails, tied the ends, and dismissed Polly to bed.

Gillian appeared shortly after to put out the lights, and see that they were all right. She went the rounds; tucked them all in; told Stacie that if her back was worse during the night to be sure to call her; and then switched off the lights, and went back to the common room for another hour of free time.

Polly had fully intended to lie awake, but nature was too strong for her, and by nine o'clock she was sound asleep, and slept through Gillian's coming to bed, and the murmured conversation she had with Stacie and Matron when the latter arrived to see how her patient was. Stacie's back still ached, but the hours of quiet and darkness were beginning to have a little effect, and by the time the last of the staff had retired to her room, and the house was in darkness, she too was sleeping quietly.

It was with a sudden jerk that Polly finally awoke, shortly after midnight. At first, she couldn't understand why she should feel so excited. Then she remembered, and hopped out of bed as speedily and silently as she could. She drew aside her cubicle curtain, and fumbled cautiously for the door-handle. She found it at last, and opened the door. Polly slipped out, and then stood still. The guidelight at one end of the corridor shed a faint glow over everything, and the full moon, peeping in through the windows at either end, lit up the narrow passage. It was all very still and rather eerie, but Polly was plucky enough, and once she had got her bearings, she made straight for the bell ropes.

They were looped up, out of the way, but Polly was tall and also agile. She made an upward spring, clutched at the loop of the rope, and brought the end down, setting the bell pealing as she did so. In all her life, Polly had never heard such a noise as that bell made! It clanged out sonorously as if it meant to rouse the whole valley – *as indeed, it did!*

No one had explained to Polly that when the bell was established, it had been arranged that it should be a signal not merely to the school, but to the whole of Briesau. The result of its sudden call through the still night over the sleeping valley can be better imagined than described! The good people of Briesau, wakened violently by that clangour, at once imagined that something direful had happened – perhaps the stream flooding.

Whatever it was, it must be something bad, and they all tumbled out of bed, and hurried to their doors to find out what was happening. The men flung on their clothes and rushed off to the Chalet. The women hastened out to see that cattle and poultry were safe, and got the stoves going. Some went down to the stream, but it was obvious that nothing was wrong there. It was full after all the rain, but not more full than usual at this time of year. Plainly, it wasn't a flood. Sadly puzzled, they returned to their homes, to wake up to the fact that the bell had ceased ringing almost as soon as it had begun. What *could* this mean?

Meanwhile, at the school, there was turmoil. Rudely wakened from their sleep, the girls tumbled out of bed, some of them screaming, others rushing to look for the fire which, they imagined, must have broken out. The staff hurriedly called them to order, saw that they were wrapped up, and marched them downstairs, and out into the playing field, where the moon looked down on a good many funny sights. For some people wore their coats with bedroom slippers; others had on dressing gowns and Wellingtons; Mademoiselle Lachenais appeared in a slumbernet, with her face thickly smeared with cold cream; Matron had tied on her apron over her dressing gown.

It was quite clear that there was no fire, so they were all marched back to the houses, by which time the men of the valley were beginning to thunder at the doors of the Chalet, demanding to know why the alarm had been rung. Nobody knew, so nobody could tell them. The only thing to do was to tell them that nothing was wrong –

an accident must have occurred. They were asked to let everyone living in the valley know as soon as possible.

Meanwhile, the staff had their hands full, trying to get their excited charges quieted and in bed again. Matron bade the maids of the various houses prepare jorums of hot milk, and then set about dosing every person within her own jurisdiction with cinnamon and quinine as a precaution against cold. Matron Venables of St Clare's and Matron Gould of St Agnes' took the same measures, and various people spoke their minds plainly about "the ass who thought it *funny* to ring the alarm!" to quote Joey.

By the time hot milk and the medicines of the three matrons had been choked down, most people were sound asleep again. Only Stacie Benson, whose back was aching worse than ever as a result of the excitement, and Polly Heriot, who was beginning to feel thoroughly frightened at what she had done, were awake when Mademoiselle came to the Green Dormitory in the course of her rounds. She spoke a few words of sympathy to Stacie, telling her not to trouble, but to sleep if she could. Then she went into the cubicle by the door. There she found a very wide-awake Polly, who looked at her with big, scared eyes, afraid of what she might be going to say. But Mademoiselle had no idea that the author of the alarm was lying before her, and she only tucked the child in, bidding her go to sleep and forget all about it. Then she went out, switching off the light, and Polly was left to make what she could of the night.

And that was very little. Matron came in to attend to Stacie three or four times, and though she was almost noiseless in her movements, Polly's conscience was so active that she scarcely slept at all and woke at the least sound. It was six o'clock before she finally slept properly and when Matey made her rounds to discover what casualties the exploit of the night had brought, she found the child sleeping so heavily, and looking so weary, that she considerately left her to have her sleep out. Consequently, it was well on for noon before Polly woke to the new day and the consequences of her own idiotic behaviour.

CHAPTER 10

Consequences

Mademoiselle had very little to say at Prayers next morning. For one thing, several of the girls were still in bed, Matey having decided to let them have their sleep out.

"I have brought a list of those who must stay where they are till they wake of themselves, so I have asked that no bells shall be rung," she had said to Mademoiselle early that morning. "Some of these people were worn out before they finally dropped off this morning; and in any case Stacie Benson must stay where she is for the next day or two. We don't want her thrown back again for want of a little care."

Mademoiselle quite agreed with this dictum, so she merely nodded, and the girls were left. Polly was sleeping soundly now and it was not until Matron peeped in again at about half-past eleven that she stirred.

Then, just as the kindly domestic tyrant of the school was about to withdraw, Polly rolled over on to her back and opened her eyes.

"Well," said Matron briskly, coming into the cubicle, "I hope you've had a long enough sleep! How do you feel this morning?"

"All right, thank you," said Polly, bewildered.

"Ready for breakfast? Then I'll send you something. It won't be much, for Mittagessen will be ready in another hour-and-a-half; but some milk and bread-and-butter won't hurt you."

"Thank you, Matron," said Polly, still rather fogged, since she was not yet properly awake. "What time is it, please?"

"Just after half-past eleven. Don't worry! You aren't the only one, by a long way. Joey Bettany was still asleep when I looked in on her ten minutes ago; and Cornelia Flower was just rousing. Be as quiet as you can, though. Stacie is in the window cubicle, and though she's awake, she is feeling rather washed-out, what with the pain in her back, and the shock of last night's affair."

Polly roused up finally at that. "*Oh!* I'd forgotten all about it!" she exclaimed.

Matron hushed her. "I told you to be quiet. Stacie has had some breakfast, and I'm hoping she may get to sleep again. That's her best medicine at present. Now lie still till you've had something to eat, and then you can get up if you like. You seem all right – quite cool, and quite refreshed now."

With that, she withdrew, and Polly was left to face the fact that there would certainly be inquiries about the night's affair, and that equally certainly she need not hope to get off scot-free. The only thing that worried her was what would her punishment be? No one would take a lenient view of such wrongdoing as hers. And – *what* had Matey said about Stacie? Was she really ill? Polly knew Stacie's story, for Cornelia Flower had told her about it. Oh! Just supposing all the excitement of last night should have upset her so badly that she had to lie still on her back again for months and months!

The bare idea upset Polly so much, that the tears came, but she choked them back resolutely. The thing was done and couldn't be undone. Crying wouldn't help matters.

Fortunately for her, the door opened, and Gredel came in, bearing a tray with a plate of bread-and-butter and a glass of milk. She smiled at Polly as she brought her tray to the bedside; but she had very little English, and Polly's command of German was almost nil. She sat up and took the tray with a shy "Danke sehr!" and Gredel went off again to her other work.

After drinking her milk and eating her bread-and-butter, Polly got up and was fully dressed by the time Matron came back a little later. Stacie was sleeping quietly again so Matron sent Polly down to the common room (since it was no use sending her into school for half-an-hour or so), and then went to see if Jo was still asleep.

In the common room Polly found Alixe von Elsen, who looked heavy-eyed and white, and Gillian Linton, who had gone in to lessons but had been forced to plead a headache halfway through the morning. These two greeted the newcomer with languid interest, and Polly sat down, wondering when she could see Mademoiselle and confess what she had done.

That didn't happen till after Mittagessen. Everyone was down by that time except Stacie. Matron declared she had better remain in bed for the next few days. Her back had been aching on and off for three days now, as she duly confessed, but she hated to seem complaining, so had said nothing about it.

"Well, Stacie," said Matron in the end, "I think you have been exceedingly foolish. I know that Dr Jem told you that you must be careful for a long time to come; and to go on with an aching back was certainly not being careful. Now you have to stay where you are for the rest of the week, whereas, if you had only told Matron Venables

111

when it began, a few hours of lying down might have made all the difference.

"It was only that I didn't want to be a nuisance," began Stacie.

"I dare say; but you're much more of a nuisance now! Now don't begin to cry," for Stacie's grey eyes were filling, "for *that* will only upset you, and it won't improve matters. I'll shake up your pillows, and move you – there! – and you must try to sleep again. But the next time your back aches, just have the sense to go straight to Matron and tell her. What do you think she's here for, if not to look after you people?" And with this, Matey, whose bark was always a good deal worse than her bite, tucked in the weary girl with a gentle hand, and then left her.

Meanwhile, in the Speisesaal, where Mittagessen had just finished, Mademoiselle was standing, looking very serious.

"Last night, the alarm bell was rung," she said gravely in French, which happened to be the language for the day. "It could not have rung of itself, and no outsider could have done it. Therefore, I wish to know if you girls know anything about it." She glanced across to where Alixe von Elsen was sitting, for Alixe had a reputation that made the mistresses pitch on her at once as the most likely person to cause trouble. But for once, Alixe was looking just a very normal little girl, and not a plaster-saint, which was what generally gave her away. Joey Bettany had once declared that when Alixe looked extra angelic, she had inevitably been up to something very much the other way.

"What is it? What is she saying?" whispered Polly anxiously to Cornelia Flower, who was sitting next to her.

"Asking who rang the alarm bell, of course," said Cornelia. "Hi! What are you up to now?"

Her question was left unanswered, for Polly had jumped up from her seat, and was making her way, terrified but determined, to where the justly incensed Head of the Chalet School was standing.

"Polly!" exclaimed the amazed lady. "What then have you to say?"

Luckily, she spoke in English, for by this time all Polly knew was that she must own up at once, and she certainly had no wits left for any language but her own.

"Please, Mademoiselle, it was me," stammered the culprit.

"*You!*" Mademoiselle sounded as if she could scarcely believe her ears.

"Yes, please." Polly was petrified, but knew she must confess. In her beloved books, either the heroine came in for a tremendous wigging, or else the Head was unable to stop laughing.

Mademoiselle did neither of these things. She looked at Polly with such a startled face, that Polly, nervy already, could only keep herself from laughing by beginning to repeat in her mind the multiplication-table. The result was funnier than anything she had anticipated.

"Polly, my child, do you understand what you are saying?" Mademoiselle asked.

And Polly answered swiftly, "Yes, Mademoiselle. Seven nines are sixty-three." Which certainly gave Mademoiselle some reason for wondering if she were quite normal!

Luckily, Miss Annersley recognized the signs. Indeed, twenty-odd years ago, when she herself had been a very naughty Middle – who *would* have thought it of Miss Annersley – she had often been reduced to the same expedient herself.

"I think, Mademoiselle," she said in her soft voice, "that Polly is speaking the truth, but that she is a little – upset."

Mademoiselle nodded. "Go to the study," she said slowly. "Wait there till I come to you."

Thankful for the respite, Polly fled, and by the time the Head put in an appearance, she had recovered her self-control.

Mademoiselle sat down by the stove. "Now, my child, please begin at the beginning, and tell me this little history," she said.

"I – er – rang the bell for – for a joke," stammered Polly.

"But – *Why?*"

Polly felt that she couldn't exactly tell her headmistress that all her favourite book heroines were always doing such things – and getting away with it as a rule, so she was tongue-tied.

Mademoiselle looked gravely at her. "I must know the reason for this so foolish piece of mischief, Polly. It was a very stupid and wrong thing to do. Apart from the fact that you roused the whole valley – and I am willing to believe that, since you are new, you did not know that our alarm bell is also meant for everyone in Briesau – you disturbed the entire school, including Stacie Benson, who has been suffering with her back for a few days, and several of the girls who are inclined to be nervous. This was very thoughtless and unkind of you, and I wish to know why you did it."

"I – I didn't know about Stacie's back," began Polly. Then she stopped. She *had* known. Matron and Bill had both said something about it, but she had been so excited over her own plans that she had thought no more of it. Being truthful by instinct as well as training, she corrected herself at once. "Yes; I *did* know; but I never thought of it at all. But I didn't know it would wake up the whole valley, Mademoiselle; truthfully, I didn't."

"Yes; I felt sure of that," said Mademoiselle. "But why did you *do* it, Polly?"

"I – I don't know."

"But, my child, you must have had a reason."

Polly fidgeted with her fingers, which she had interlaced behind her back. This interview wasn't following the approved lines at all. If Mademoiselle had given her a sharp scolding and ended up with a still sharper punishment, Polly could have understood that. But this serious talk spiked her guns. Mademoiselle, having no clue to the mystery, sat back and looked at her; and Polly, her head hanging down, shifted from one foot to the other, and felt supremely silly.

It was left to Mademoiselle to win the trick. Rising, she said, still in that grave, rather impassive voice, "You will stay here till you are given permission to go, Polly." And she left the room, closing the door quietly.

Polly stared after her wide-eyed. Was this to be her punishment – imprisonment in the study? And must she remain standing all the time, or might she venture to sit down? She wasn't sure, and she didn't quite dare to take it for granted; so when Joey Bettany entered the room, her face very grave (though her eyes danced with a wicked light), the prisoner was still standing where the Head had left her.

Joey strolled across the room to the swivel chair before the big desk and sat herself down. "Now then, come here and tell me what all this means," she ordered calmly.

It was very much what Mademoiselle had said; but Joey was a different sort of person. She wasn't so far from her own schooldays that she wouldn't understand, and Polly felt this. She crossed the room till she was standing by the desk, and facing Jo.

"It – it was the – school stories," she faltered.

"School stories?" exclaimed Joey, a slight flush coming over her face. She knew the type of book which had inspired Polly, but she still couldn't understand exactly what the child meant, and she fully intended to do so before she had finished. "What in the world had school stories to do with you doing such a mad thing?" she asked.

Polly flushed. Somehow, now that it was all over and she was facing the music, what she had done didn't seem either so funny or so clever as she had thought. "It – those girls – they – did things like that," she got out.

Jo shaped her lips to a silent whistle of surprise. "Do you really mean to say that just because the heroines of your favourite form of literature do insane things, you feel you've got to copy them to keep your end up?" She exclaimed. "I didn't think a sensible kid like you could be so idiotic on occasion!"

As this was exactly what Polly had felt, she said nothing; but she felt quite as idiotic as Jo had called her.

"What possessed you to do it last night of all nights, anyhow?" pursued Joey. "I should have thought you would have realized that the staff had quite enough on their hands, thanks to that ceiling coming down, without *you* adding to their troubles."

"That was why," murmured Polly.

"*What?*"

Polly explained. "You see, I'd thought of doing it ages ago only it didn't seem possible to get from St Clare's to Ste Thérèse's without waking anyone. And when we were sent over here, and I was put right up at the top, next door to the bell rope, it – it seemed an opportunity."

"I see!" Jo mused over this for a few minutes. "Well, you've made a howling ass of yourself. And if your idea was to make yourself popular, you've gone the wrong way about it. You've made Mademoiselle look a fool before the valley; you've upset two or three people, including Stacie, pretty badly; and you've hauled us all out of bed on a freezing night for no good reason. If you think that sort of thing amuses us here, you're vastly mistaken, and so you'll find out before you're much older. Well, I've nothing more to say to you. Wait a moment! Yes, I have! You can give my compliments to whoever is junior librarian, and ask her to give you *Stalky and Co.,* by Kipling, and you can read it – every word of it. And you can just read, mark, learn, and inwardly digest what the Three have to say about old Prout. Now I'm going to tell this extraordinary rigmarole of yours to Mademoiselle. You'd better sit down till she comes to you, when she'll probably give you her own opinion of your conduct." Joey rose and left the room, leaving a completely deflated Polly behind her.

Nor was she much cheered up by the subsequent interview with Mademoiselle, who told her that she had expected better things of a girl of her age. She was to read the book Joey had recommended, and she was to take all her possessions downstairs to the observation room, which opened out of Matron's.

That was all; but it was quite enough. It was a very crushed young person who crept from the room, and went, as Joey had commanded, to ask meekly if Arda van der Windt would give her *Stalky and Co.*

Nor did it end there. Many of the girls were decidedly cross at being hauled out of bed for nothing, and they told Polly plainly what they thought of her. Finally the immortal Trio's views on the subject of "Popularity Prout" completed her demoralization.

As for Jo, she sat down that afternoon to review her own book, and with a stern hand she remorselessly removed any pranks that might be supposed to incite brainless Juniors to imitation.

"Matey was quite right," she thought, as she consigned the last sheet to the wastepaper basket. "What a horrible responsibility it is to write for the young!"

CHAPTER 11

Trouble for the Chalet School

It is certain that Polly would have heard much more from
the school about her latest exploit if it had not been for
what happened next. As it was, she had to endure a good
deal of ragging from her own clan for the next two or three
days. But then something occurred which put all thoughts
of the alarm bell out of their heads. Mademoiselle fell ill.

It was a rare thing indeed for the Head of the school
to be ill. She rarely even suffered from a head cold.
So when, one morning, Miss Annersley not only took
Frühstück, but also read Prayers, the girls were thoroughly
startled. They knew that Mademoiselle had not gone to
the Sonnalpe, for four people had been sent to her at
nineteen hours the night before to explain – if they could!
– why they had spent a good part of preparation in playing at noughts-and-crosses instead of going on with their
work. Renée Lecoutier, Elma Conroy, Emmie Linders,
and Gretchen Braun had reported on their return to St
Clare's that Mademoiselle had been "at her most severe",
and had given them such a lecture on wasting their time as
they had never had from her before. Therefore, when Miss
Annersley, as senior mistress, went to the reading desk on
the hall platform at Prayers, they wondered what could
have happened.

They were to know soon enough. When Prayers were
over Miss Annersley told everyone that Mademoiselle had
been ill all night, and would certainly not be in school for

119

the next day or two. In the meantime, it was hoped that the girls would be very quiet, so as not to disturb her. That was all. She sent them off to their form rooms after that, where they settled to work, rather overawed.

Mademoiselle remained very poorly for the rest of the week, and Miss Stewart, who had not been looking well, went down with a severe attack of laryngitis on the following Monday.

"There's no help for it, Jo," said Miss Annersley, as the staff, with Joey, were having their Kaffee und Kuchen. "You'll have to take history for the entire Middle School. Polly Heriot must just do without your private lessons, and manage as well as she can in form with the others. I can take on Senior history myself; and Miss Carey has had all the Juniors since she came; so it might be worse. If you'll take on the Middles, I think we can manage. But I can't do more than the Seniors. Neither Miss Wilson nor Miss Nalder could give us help in that subject, and Miss Leslie says she can't. We seem to have a painfully mathematically-minded staff! Can you undertake Third, the two Fourths, and Five B? It should be only for a week or two."

"I can manage all right if I haven't to worry over Polly's coaching," said Jo sturdily. "I don't know that I'd care to tackle either of the Sixths or Five A," she added, with a laugh. "After all, some of the Sixths were in the same form with me only last term. How is Miss Stewart, by the way?"

"Very poorly indeed," said Miss Wilson. "It is a sharp attack, and she can neither swallow nor speak at present. She's worrying, too, about the work, as Mademoiselle is *hors de combat* as well; and that's not good for her."

"You can tell her not to worry since Joey and I can

see to the work between us," said Miss Annersley sympathetically. "Besides, Matey has rung up the Sonnalpe,
and I expect someone from there this evening."

"It's a sweet night if he's coming by the mountain
path," said Jo. "Just listen to that!" And they heard
the rising wind drive the heavy rain against the closed
shutters. "If this goes on, we'll be having a second flood.
I don't remember such a wet autumn in all the years I've
lived here!"

"Don't worry! It can't go on much longer," said Miss
Leslie. "We are very nearly into November now; so the
snows can't be delayed much longer."

"If it comes on top of this it won't be snow – it'll
be mud," said Miss Wilson pessimistically.

"If the rain would only cease, that wind would soon dry
up things," declared Miss Nalder. "Don't worry, Nell! We
never get much in the way of mud here."

"Well," said Miss Annersley, "to revert to the earlier
subject of our conversation. I'll send the form prefect of
each form to you with their textbooks and notes, Joey, and
you can see what they've been doing with Miss Stewart.
And that reminds me. They must try not to call you by
your baptismal name while you are teaching them. You
will be a member of the staff for the time being, and they
must treat you as such."

Joey nearly dropped her coffee cup at this. "Oh, Miss
Annersley! You surely don't want them to call me 'Miss
Bettany'? I stopped even Polly doing it – it makes me feel
such an awful ass!"

The staff chuckled. This was Jo all over.

Miss Annersley considered the point for a moment or
two. "It's a difficult proposition, Jo. Well, so long as they
behave with you as they would with any other member of

the staff, I'll let it go, as you are so much against it. But if they start taking liberties with 'Jo', it will have to be 'Miss Bettany', I'm afraid, whatever it makes you feel."

"Besides, you've got to be it some day soon," added Miss Leslie. "You aren't a baby any longer now, you know."

"Oh, I don't mind outsiders," acknowledged Jo. "It's the school doing it that I object to. Why, Thora, and Anne, and Luigia, and the rest were in form with me last term. I simply couldn't expect them to 'Miss Bettany' me all over the place – and I should hate it, too," she added with decision.

"Well, we'll leave it at that," said Miss Annersley, rising. "Any more coffee, anyone? No? Then ring the bell, someone, to have all this cleared away. I must get back to my own quarters. The bell should be ringing for prep, shortly. Joey, where will you be?"

"In the staff room, I suppose," said Joey with a groan. "I'd better not go back to my own room, in case I get buried in *Cecily*. Which table do I bag, please?"

"You'd better have Miss Stewart's," said Miss Wilson. "Don't sling the ink over it – that's all we ask of you."

With another heartfelt sigh, Joey got up, and retired to the staff room over at Ste Thérèse's, to where came presently Thelma Johansen, Kitty Burnett, and Bette Schmaltz, the respective heads of the three top forms of the Middle School. Jeanne le Cadoulec of Five B arrived a little later. They all brought copies of their textbooks; and the two elder girls had notebooks with the notes Miss Stewart had dictated to them as well. They left these with Joey, after explaining what they had been doing lately, and then departed to their own work.

Jo looked at the heap before her, clutched her head,

122

much to the detriment of her hair, and groaned loudly. "Oh, what a fearful business!"

"Nonsense!" laughed Miss Leslie, the only other occupant of the staff room at the time. "It'll do you good, my child – teach you to feel a little sympathy for your former mistresses!"

"They're all at different stages," groaned Jo, turning over the pile of books before her. "And every form uses a different textbook. If only they were all at the same period, it wouldn't be so bad – or if it were only history of *one* country. History of Europe is such an all-embracing subject!"

"It's not as bad as all that," said Miss Leslie, taking pity on her, and coming over to see what was happening.

A few kindly words and helpful hints born of experience soon put Jo at her ease, and in a few minutes Miss Leslie retired to her table, and Jo set to work to evolve a test which later made a good many people groan when they saw it. She managed very well next day, for the Third Form still regarded her rather in the light of the Head Girl she had been, and were on their best behaviour. Four A were still at the mark-hunting age and too keen to make nuisances of themselves. Jo enjoyed the lesson with the younger girls. She went to the staff room after morning school feeling quite pleased with herself.

"What about this afternoon?" she asked anxiously. "There doesn't seem to be any work down."

"Miss Stewart was on walk duty," said Miss Annersley, "but," with a glance at the streaming panes, "I'm afraid walks are definitely off. The Middles will do prep instead, with you to supervise, and have the evening free. You can do your own work then, Joey. What have you tomorrow?"

"Nothing for the first two periods, as you are taking

the Sixths. I have Five B for the third hour, though; and Four B for the fourth."

"And the afternoon?"

"Miss Stewart has private coaching written across it, and a lot of initials," said Jo, puckering her brows over the timetable.

"Let me see!" Miss Annersley took the sheet and studied it thoughtfully. "Yes – that's Gillian Linton and Louise Redfield. They are doing your own special period – the Napoleonic era. You could manage that quite well, couldn't you? I'd advise you to find out exactly what they are doing, and put in an hour's reading unless you happen to have it at your fingertips. But as you have the whole of the first half of the morning free, that should be no trouble."

"No-o," said Jo.

"This second period is Stacie Benson, Joyce Linton, and Irma Ancokzky. I happen to know that they are having special coaching on the Wars of the Holy League. Do you think you could take it on?"

Jo nodded. "Rather! I've been reading it up lately, and I really do know something about it. So I'll take them, too, shall I?"

"Yes, please, Joey. I would take them myself, but I have one of Mademoiselle's French translation coachings then, and that mustn't go. I know that Gillian and Louise, at least, could be trusted to work on alone – possibly, even the other three. But if you *can* take them on, it would be a blessing. And, while I think of it, I'd rather you set them all as little written work as possible."

"Would you?" asked Jo doubtfully. "You know, even slackers do more at written work than at learning, as a rule."

"Oh, I know that, but I think you'll find plenty to

do without giving yourself piles of essays and exercises to correct. Finally, there is your own special work. I don't know how far you are on with that book of yours, Jo, but we are all expecting great things from it, and you must get on with it. Just think what a glorious finish it would be to the term if we could announce that a publisher had accepted it!"

"That's not too likely," said Jo. "Oh, it's finished now, and I meant to ask if I might borrow the typewriter from the study. But I doubt if any publisher will ever take it."

"Don't be pessimistic, Jo! After all, you can but try!"

"Well, I mean to. But you know the saying, 'Happy is he who expecteth nothing, for he won't be disappointed.' I've made up my mind not to break my heart if it is turned down all round. Anyway, *may* I borrow the typewriter, Miss Annersley?"

"Of course. I don't think you'd better take it out of the study; but no one is likely to be there in the evenings, which is when you want to use it, I suppose?"

"Yes; that's what I'd thought of doing," agreed Jo. "I really must coax Jem and Madge to give me one for Christmas. I shall need it if I'm to go on with this sort of thing."

Miss Annersley nodded. "Yes; that's true. Come in! Yes, Gredel? What is it?"

"The Herr Bettany and Frau Bettany wish to see Fräulein Bettany," said Gredel, a stolid Tyrolean peasant, of whom Cornelia Flower had once said that if you tied jumping-crackers to her skirts and let them all off at once, she would never turn a hair.

Up jumped Jo, and away went her red ink – she had been correcting the Fourth Form tests. Luckily the ink was in a safety-pot, so no harm was done; but Miss Annersley felt that she had done the right thing in forbidding Jo to set much written work for her forms.

"Dick and Mollie here?" cried the author of the accident. "Sorry, Miss Annersley! Luckily, it can't spill! Where are they, Gredel?"

"Sie sind im Salon, mein Fräulein," replied Gredel.

"Excuse me, *please*, Miss Annersley," begged Joey, making for the door. "I simply *must* see what they want! I hope there's nothing wrong at the Sonnalpe!"

The last part of her speech came from a distance as she fled down the corridor, took the stairs in about four bounds, and entered the salon, out of breath and untidy.

"Well, you imp," said her brother severely, as he kissed her, "we heard you coming! What's all this rigmarole Miss Wilson has been unloading on to us? You teaching history?"

"Sure, Dick, be quiet, will you, and give the poor creature a chance to speak!" protested his wife, as she took her turn in the embraces. "Joey, mavourneen, we've come to say goodbye to you."

"*What*?" Jo stared. "Say goodbye? But I thought you had another three weeks before you had to move?"

"So we have," said Dick, as they all sat down. "The bother is that, as you know, we want to take the overland route to Port Said, for the Mediterranean seems to be suffering from the jimjams, if all one hears is true, and Mollie still remains the world's worst sailor. All this wretched rain and the gales we are having seem to be putting the railway out of action temporarily, so we feel we'd better get off and not risk missing the boat. We've been spending the last two days in Innsbruck, saying farewell to all we know, and we're taking you in on the way back, for we're off

126

on Thursday, and there won't be time to get down again, I'm afraid."

"And if there was, d'you think I'm leaving my babies a minute I don't have to?" demanded his wife.

"Yes – where is Jack?" asked Joey, looking all round, rather as if she expected to find her youngest nephew adorning a shelf or the picture rail. "What have you done with him?"

"He's at Die Rosen, of course. You don't imagine we were going to let a ten months' baby in for a succession of Kaffeeklatschen, do you?" queried Dick, suddenly graver.

Mollie turned to her young sister-in-law and said, with a choke in her voice, "Sure, Joey, you may as well know first as last. Jack is staying here. We aren't taking him back with us."

"But – I thought you'd decided as he was so young another three years or so wouldn't hurt him," said Joey in bewildered tones.

"True for you. We did so. But Jem says he's doing so well here 'twould be a pity to risk upsetting him by taking him back there again. And then – well, there's to be another little brother or sister for them at the end of next April, and Jackie would be just the age when he was one person's work. So, as Madge, bless her, said she'd be a mother to him, the same as she is to the rest, we decided it would be best to leave him where he is," said Mollie.

Dick hurriedly changed the subject. "Now, then, Moll! Where've you put that little case?"

"Och, yes! Your birthday gift, Joey!" cried Mollie with one of the mercurial changes which were so characteristic of her Irish temperament. "Listen, mavourneen. Madge told us about the book you're writing, and Dick and I wanted to give you a really decent present, for it'll have

127

to be birthday and Christmas in one, since we're not likely to reach Bombay before Christmas Day. So we went to Innsbruck to get it for you, and there it is – by the settee yonder, in that case."

With a whoop, Joey was on the case pointed out and unlocking the clasps. A moment later, and she uttered a wild shriek of joy, for there lay one of the desires of her heart – a portable typewriter!

"Neat but not gaudy," said her brother, with a grin. "Also a delicate hint that a few more letters would be acceptable, and this gives you no excuse for not writing. Do you like it?"

Like it? Jo was far too overcome to tell him what she really felt. But her flushed face and sparkling eyes spoke for her, and satisfied the generous donors. They had provided paper, ribbons, rubber, dusters, and everything they could think of.

"You dears!" she cried ecstatically. "What a gorgeous present!"

"It'll save Jem's temper, anyhow," said his brother-in-law, submitting to being hugged vehemently. "I can just imagine what he'd feel like if he happened to want to use his typewriter and found you'd lugged it off to your own room!"

"Yes," said Jo calmly. "I was going to use that as a good reason why he and Madge should give me a portable for Christmas. However, I needn't now. Mollie, as soon as I've done the copy of *Cecily* to send away, I'll type you one, too, and send it to India, so that you don't have to wait for it to be published – if it ever is! – before you read it."

"But don't you think that'll get you out of sending us a copy when it *is* published, Miss!" said her brother severely. "You needn't think we intend to be fobbed off with a typewritten copy. By the way, can you use the thing?"

Joey nodded. "Oh yes! I used to get up early in the summer and sneak down to the office and practise on Jem's. He wondered why on earth he was using so much typing paper," she added, with her most impish grin.

"The wonder is he didn't catch you," said Mollie.

"He very nearly did one morning. I had to nip into that cupboard where he hangs his things, and I thought he was never going. By the way, have you two had Kaffee und Kuchen?"

"You're rather late with your hospitalities, aren't you?" demanded Dick. "Of course we have – had it in Spärtz before we came on up here."

"Are you staying the night?" Joey had forgotten the illness at the Chalet.

"No, Joey," said her sister-in-law gently. "We couldn't be doing that with Miss Stewart and Mademoiselle ill. We've got a car outside, and we're driving round. So we must be going now. We've seen Margot and Daisy and Stacie. We left you to the last. Come and kiss me goodbye, Joey."

Jo raised dismayed eyes. "Going already? But Mollie! You'll be away another three years! Can't you possibly stay, just for tonight?"

"No, we can't," said her brother curtly. "As you say, we'll be away for three years, and – well, we're leaving the kiddies behind."

"I'd forgotten that," said Jo remorsefully. "Oh, Dick, I wish you weren't in India! It's so gorgeous having you and Mollie with us, and India is so far away!"

"Rot!" he said, somewhat roughly. He cut the farewells

short. He knew his wife too well to risk a storm of tears, and it seemed to Jo that they had barely come before they had gone, and she was left to go back to the salon to collect her newest treasure and cart it back up to her room. There she disposed of it on the table very breathlessly, and then examined it, and slipping in a sheet of paper, typed the title page of her new book.

CECILY HOLDS THE FORT
BY
JOSEPHINE M. BETTANY

It did look nice! The only thing that would look nicer would be the title page of the printed book. Joey forgot all about history, her form, and everything else. She sat down before that wonderful machine, and when the gong rang for Abendessen, she had her first chapter typed out.

CHAPTER 12

Livening Things Up a Little

For the next week or so, things went on quietly. Mademoiselle recovered more or less – chiefly less – from her indisposition, and came into school to take Prayers and see to its organization. But she was not permitted to teach. The doctors from the Sonnalpe forbade it most positively. Miss Stewart, who had had a very sharp attack, was still far from well, and was kept in the little sanatorium which lay at the far end of St Clare's, divided from the workaday part of the school. News from Die Rosen continued to be much the same. Whooping cough had not spread beyond Master Rix, fortunately; but he was having an unpleasant time of it, and his Aunt Madge reported that he was very fretful and tiresome.

Frieda Mensch came up from Innsbruck to spend a few days, and she was promptly pressed into service by the staff, taking French and German among the Juniors, who were thrilled at being taught by Frieda. Unfortunately, she had only been there four days when Frau Mensch wrote to beg her to come home. Frau Mensch's sister had slipped on the stairs and sprained her ankle badly. So Frieda had to pack up and return to Innsbruck, which she did with a good deal of reluctance.

Meanwhile, Polly, having decided to shelve adventures for the present, had struck up a tremendous friendship with Joyce Linton, who was rather more than a year older than herself. In this way, she came under the influence of Joyce's sister, Gillian, who was noted throughout the school for her quiet common sense. She was not likely to encourage Polly in any wild fancies, and Joyce was also on her best behaviour, so the folk in authority allowed themselves to breathe freely.

As for Jo, she plunged as deeply into the typing of her precious book as circumstances would permit. *Cecily Holds the Fort* was the pride of her heart at the moment. She had taken Matron's advice, and her characters were neither diabolically bad nor angelically good, but just normal girls of the type she met every day. She had expunged the one or two most startling adventures of her heroine after Polly's exploit, and Matron, who had insisted that she should be privileged to read it, was of the private opinion that it would most certainly find a publisher somewhere. Jo had a crisp, racy style of her own, and she could tell a story well. Cecily was remarkably well drawn; and as for the science mistress, Matron gurgled over *her* most reprehensively, for Jo had reproduced Bill to the life.

"Well, you're getting on with it," Matron said on the night of Frieda's return home. "How much more have you left to do?"

"Oh, about seven chapters," said Jo. "I don't know when you'll get the rest to read, for I certainly shan't get at it again before Saturday. Now that Frieda has had to go home, I've offered to take over her classes where they don't clash with my own. However, I'll have the whole of Saturday after Guides, and that ought to see me through at least two more, and with luck I'll get the rest done next week. Then it'll have to be packed off, and after that, I'll have to wait and hope for the best, I suppose."

"Where are you sending it?" asked Matron curiously.

Jo mentioned the name of a well-known firm, and Matron nodded. "I know them. They publish a good many books for children. I should think *Cecily* will have quite a good chance with them. Well, I must go now. I've got all the household linen from the laundry to go through." She turned, and went to the door. Arrived there, she swung round, facing Jo squarely. "You've been a brick through all this trouble, Jo," she said bluntly. "The staff would have managed somehow, I suppose; but your taking on all this teaching has helped them tremendously."

"I dare say!" said Jo sceptically. "Anyone who likes it can have the job for all of me! I wasn't born to be a teacher, Matey. And I don't mind telling *you* that I hoped to have had that book off before this. As it is, I doubt if I shall hear anything of it till next year. Publishers must be frantically busy about Christmas, sending off all the piles and piles of books they must to the shops. I did hope I'd know something definite about it this term."

"Never mind! You've had an experience that will probably be very useful to you later on," said Matron soothingly. "By the way, when do they expect you back at Die Rosen?"

"Barring accidents, a fortnight after half term. That will give Miss Stewart and Mademoiselle time to pull themselves together, and I shan't be needed then, so I can go with a free mind. The girls are all saying there'll be little more than three weeks left of the term, and I might as well stay and see it out; but – Mercy! What's that?"

"That" was a crash which sounded as though someone had dropped a bomb through the roof. Matron dropped the clean towels she had been carrying and scurried off, followed at top speed by Jo, both sure that, at the very least, some part of the house must have collapsed.

Guided by the sound of excited voices, they reached the common room, where they found at least half the house standing round one girl, who was getting up from the floor with a rather dazed expression in her eyes, and a rapidly rising bump on her forehead.

"Well, Cornelia," said Matron, "what have you been doing this time?"

At the sound of her voice, the throng parted, and she advanced on the unlucky Cornelia, who had managed to gain her feet.

"What have you been doing?" repeated Matron, as she examined the lump. "We heard the crash in Jo's room, and I thought that at least the roof had fallen in. Here; you must have this attended to at once. Give her a queen's chair, two of you. She looks shaky."

Cornelia did look shaky – but no more so than her boon companion and usual accomplice in evil, Evadne Lannis. Jo, running her eye rapidly over the scared-looking crowd, saw her white face, and as soon as the patient had been borne away by Gillian Linton and Cyrilla Maurús, beckoned to her, and demanded to know what they had all been doing.

"Corney – fell," said Evadne, who seemed, for once, to be completely deprived of her self-possession. "I say, Joey! She looked real bad. She'll be all right, won't she?"

"I don't know," said Jo truthfully. "And as for 'fell', I gathered that much for myself. What I want to know is, what on earth she was doing to fall? She must have come down with an awful crash to get a bang like that – to say nothing of the noise she made."

Evadne shuffled uncomfortably from one foot to the other.

"Go on," said Jo inflexibly. "I can guess that you

134

imps have been up to something wicked, and what it is I mean to know before any of us are very much older. So the sooner you cough it up, the better for us all!"

"We-ell," drawled Evadne at length, "Corney was just trying to go round the room without touching the floor, just as we do in the gym, you know."

"*What*?"

"Well, you know how we do it – swinging from the ropes and the wall bars. We thought we'd try it here, with the furniture, and the windowsills, and so on. If you touched the floor at all, you'd be disqualified."

"Disqualified? What on earth do you mean?"

Prodded on by Jo's questions, Evadne finally informed her that five girls had volunteered to try it, and the one who did it in the shortest time would be proclaimed winner.

"And how many of you have done it?" asked Jo with real curiosity.

"None of us. Corney was the first, because it was her idea," said Evadne. "We others were to come after in alphabetical order."

"I see. And who were the others, if you've no objection to telling me?"

"Me, of course – "

"Of course," agreed Jo. "Who else was in it?"

"Lonny – and Irma – and Giovanna. That was all."

"And quite enough, too. I'm glad the rest had more sense than you five seem to have! How did Corney happen to fall by the way?"

"It was when she was climbing from the settee to the top of the stove," explained Ilonka, pushing back her long brown plaits as she spoke. "She had one foot on the stove, and she found it was very hot – too hot to stand there. She

135

cried out, and tried to get back to the settee. I suppose the stretch was too far, for she slipped and fell backwards on that table, and they both went. I suppose that was really what made the crash. We were too frightened to notice properly. Corney looked so terrible lying there with her eyes shut, and her face white." And she shuddered.

Jo measured the distance with her eye, and shuddered too. "She might easily have been killed! What other mad things did she do?"

After severe questioning, she discovered that Cornelia's race had begun from the chair near the door. From there, she had jumped to a small table – the investigator discovered that an accident had nearly happened then, for the table was a light one, and it had rocked dangerously under the shock – and had then taken a wild leap to the nearest window seat, on which she had fallen on all-fours. From there, it had been child's play to run along the shelf, which they had cleared of the photographs and ornaments it normally held, and so, to the second window seat.

Her next feat had been to leap to the settee, along which she had strolled, and then, making a long leg, had stretched up to the top of the porcelain stove, which was kept going both day and night at this time of year. She had tried to get back to the settee when the heat struck up through the thin sole of her dancing sandal, had overbalanced, and crashed down.

"You must all have been mad!" said Jo finally. "Corney might have been killed. As it is, she's had a nasty knock, and the table is badly damaged."

"Do – do you think Corney's – likely to be real sick?" asked Evadne shakily.

"I couldn't say. She looked to me as if she had slight concussion. I didn't like that dazed look in her eyes," said

Jo gravely. She meant to frighten them, for, as she said later on, there was no saying what pranks they might play next if they weren't stopped now. Apart from that, while going round the room without touching the floor was all very well in the gymnasium, with Miss Nalder there to see that it was properly done and the mattresses in position, the same feat in the common room, with no precautions whatsoever, was a very different matter.

Evadne bit her lips and turned away. Ilonka turned a face of absolute horror on the elder girl; and Irma and Giovanna burst into tears. The rest of the throng looked very sober. Jo had convinced them that they had come very near a tragedy.

As for Jo herself, having scared them all thoroughly, she retreated to inquire after the patient and then went to her room to gather up her books before she went off to St Clare's, where she was due to take preparation.

No one at St Clare's had heard of what had been happening at Ste Thérèse's, and Jo had no intention of enlightening them. She called them to order and, spreading out the Second Form's history exercise books on the desk, settled down to some correcting. Sharp as she generally was, she had failed to notice the looks of dismay exchanged between two or three of the Middles when she entered, and beyond asking who was practising now, she took little further notice of them, once the room was quiet.

At first, all went well. The girls settled to their work, and there was comparative silence for the first half-hour. Then Enid Southern, an imp of twelve, put up her hand.

"Yes?" said Jo. "What is it, Enid?"

"Please, Jo, I can't do my algebra. I don't understand it."

"Bring it out here, then," said Jo, pushing aside her

books, and removing the red ink to a place of safety. She had no fears that she could not cope with Enid's mathematics, for that young lady had only just begun algebra, and though Jo's own work had been the despair of Miss Leslie, she knew that she could deal with the elementary rules well enough.

Enid brought out her work, and Jo carefully explained simple multiplication to her, Enid listening with perhaps half an ear. When she said she understood, she was sent back to her seat, and Jo prepared to go on with her work.

Hilda Bhaer made the next interruption. "Please, Jo, my throat feels dry. May I go and get a drink?"

"Very well. But don't be away longer than three minutes," said Jo, glancing at her watch.

Hilda saw her, and retreated with a very downcast face. She dared not stay longer than the three minutes, and the thing she had meant to do would certainly take longer than that. Jo was evidently on the warpath, so she waited in the corridor till she thought the time was up, and then returned, with a shake of her head at one or two other people, who promptly looked very crestfallen.

Biddy O'Ryan held up her hand ten minutes later. "'Tis meself doesn't know what to do with this at all,' she said, with a rich Kerry brogue, when Jo asked her what she wanted.

"Bring it out here, then – and speak decent English," added Jo. "You can when it suits you."

Biddy meekly trotted out with her French grammar, and Jo patiently explained what had to be done. Biddy listened with exemplary gravity, said she understood, and returned to her seat. Her French was returned next day, with horrified ejaculations from little Mademoiselle Lachenais.

There was peace again after that, till Mary Shaw, a small American who was famed for the fertility of her wits, proclaimed that she could not understand the poetry Jo had given them to learn for repetition. Jo called her out, elucidated her difficulties with a somewhat tart remark to the effect that, if she kept her brains for her work instead of thinking of various evil deeds, it would be better for her, and then sent her back to her seat.

An almost oppressive silence settled down on the room after that, though Jo was too much absorbed in her work to notice it. Suddenly, there came the most hair-raising sound, apparently from the middle of the room. Jo jumped violently, and one or two of the more nervous girls who were not in the secret shrieked.

But though Jo might jump when startled, she had plenty of common sense, and she guessed at once that this was merely a new effort on the part of the Middles to liven things up a little.

"Who made that noise?" she demanded sharply.

No answer; but one or two people giggled, and Beryl Lester, a highly strung child in the Fourth, burst into tears, wailing, "Please, Jo, it wasn't me! I never did it!"

"I didn't for a moment imagine you did, Beryl," said Jo. "Stop that babyish crying, please. Well?" This last being addressed to the room at large.

There was a dead silence. No one would confess to being the author of the sound, and even as she waited for an answer, it came again. Two or three more nervy people started. Joey decided that this must *cease*!

"All of you put down whatever you have in your hands, and sit back with your arms folded behind you," she said.

Everyone obeyed. With Jo Bettany looking like that, they felt it to be the wisest course. When they were all sitting still, she got up and went the rounds. Halfway through the business, the noise came again, and Mary Shand, a nervy child from Louisiana, squeaked with horror. Biddy O'Ryan also gave a little gasp.

"Don't be silly," said Jo bracingly. "Someone is playing tricks – I know that. And I know another thing: you will all sit like that until whoever is responsible for it owns up."

"But, Jo! We don't know, honestly!" protested Ruth Wynyard. "And I haven't touched either my history or geometry yet."

"I can't help that. *Someone* knows what it's all about, and the innocent must suffer with the guilty, unless the guilty choose to confess and have done with it," said Jo, with her most inexorable expression.

The door opened, and three girls came in – Dorothy Brentham, a tomboyish person from Five B, Joyce Linton, and Renée Lecoutier, Mademoiselle Lepâttre's young cousin.

"Where have you all been?" demanded Jo.

"Only practising," replied Joyce, opening her eyes at the tone.

"Any others to come from practising?" continued Jo.

"Yes – Alixe von Elsen and Sigrid Bjornessen," replied Violet Allison, one of the senior Middles, after a quick glance round.

"Alixe and Sigrid – H'm!" Jo thought over the pair in her own mind. She knew Sigrid for a somewhat colourless little person, very law-abiding, and not likely to have had anything to do with this. Alixe was a different matter. She looked as though butter wouldn't melt in her mouth. She was very fair, with a misleadingly saintly expression, which got saintlier as she became more wicked. Her voice was soft and shy, and she said outrageous things in a gentle manner, which made people frequently pass over her remarks till they had had time to consider them. In Alixe's case, still waters were apt to run very deep indeed.

Not by the widest stretch of imagination could Jo picture Sigrid having taken part in this disturbance, Alixe was quite capable of it. What was more, Alixe's own particular circle were glancing at each other, and this time the elder girl was able to read deep meaning into their glances.

"Violet, you and Ruth may go and find those two and send them here," she said. "In any case, their practice time is over by now. Who is due at the pianos next?"

Five hands were raised. They all belonged to people who were more or less possessed of good characters.

"You five may go," said Jo, dismissing them. "Hurry up, and don't waste your time."

"May – may I not rise early tomorrow and do my practice then, please, Joey?" queried Inga shyly.

"Oh, nonsense, Inga! You aren't frightened by a silly trick, are you?"

"It – it is such a very horrid noise," said Inga shakily.

"I know it is. But it's most likely Alixe up to monkey tricks of some kind," said Jo soothingly. "However," she added, with an eye to Inga's white face, "if you'd rather wait a little, you may. What about the rest of you?"

"It's only someone trying to be funny," said Kitty, scorn in her voice. "*I'm* not going to funk it. Besides, it's my lesson tomorrow."

"But I do not like it either," put in Emmie in her own tongue. "Please, Joey, I would rather wait, if you do not mind."

"Very well, Emmie, though I must say I think you and

141

Inga are very silly little girls. What about you, Faith and Thelma?"

Faith and Thelma elected to go to their practice, probably moved to this decision by the fact that they, like Kitty, had lessons on the morrow. Emmie and Inga sat down again, and the people who had just come in took their seats. Two minutes later, Ruth and Violet entered, bringing Alixe and Sigrid with them. Sigrid looked startled, and Alixe wore her most seraphic air – which Jo promptly recognized as a bad sign. That the expression changed to one of shock when she saw the ex-Head Girl of the school at the mistress's desk, settled this latter young lady's mind.

"Well, and what have you people been doing?" Jo asked in chilly tones. "You were supposed to be here ten minutes ago."

"Please, Jo, my music case slipped behind the piano, and I could not get it out until Violet and Ruth came to help me," explained Sigrid, with a blush.

"I thought you people weren't supposed to put your cases on top of the pianos?" said Jo.

Sigrid went even redder, and looked at her slipper toes. "I forgot. I am very sorry."

"Well, you can come to me at the end of prep for twelve lines of repetition. Perhaps that will help you to remember," said Jo sarcastically. "And what about you, Alixe? Have *you* been trying to get your music case from behind the piano, too?"

"Oh, but *no*!" said Alixe with great fervour, though she had winced at the edge in Jo's tones.

"Then what *have* you been doing?"

"Just practising – and I had to put my music in the locker."

142

"*That* didn't take you all this time. What else? Come here."

Alixe came, her saintly expression a little less in evidence as she did so.

"Hold up your foot," said Jo sternly. "Show me your slipper sole."

Alixe no longer looked like a young saint in embryo. She was merely a very naughty little girl who had been caught out. She extended one foot reluctantly, and Jo saw, as she had suspected, that the sole of her slipper was soaking.

"So it *was* you," she said thoughtfully, as Alixe put her foot down again.

The culprit said nothing. She had not bargained for Jo being quite so sharp, though she knew, from past experience, that very little escaped that young lady. It was a nuisance that the weather had changed. The day before had been beautifully fine, and all today it had been quite dry, if somewhat grey. But with nightfall there had come up a heavy mist which had soaked everything. Besides that, Jo's quick eyes had seen a trace of gravel on the floor by the door.

"What have you been doing?" she demanded.

"It – it was only a joke," muttered Alixe sulkily, still in her own tongue.

"A very foolish joke, and one that might have startled someone very badly. How did you manage it?"

For reply, Alixe produced from her pocket one of those balloon creatures which, when blown up and then released, let out the air with unearthly screeches. Once, in the dim and distant past, Elsie Carr had brought in a similar thing to prep, and had got into serious trouble over it. But that had been *inside* the room. Jo could not

143

understand how Alixe had contrived to work hers when she had been outside all the time.

"Where were you standing?" she asked with real curiosity.

Alixe pointed. "Under that ventilator there. We found out the other day, that if anyone talks beneath it, the sounds are just as if they are in the middle of this room. I thought it would be a joke to use this thing outside it one night during prep. I did not know that you would be here instead of Anne," she finished in injured tones.

Joey nearly collapsed at this, but she managed to keep a tight grip on herself, and only looked very stern and judicial. "I see. Well, you have brought your own punishment on yourself. You can go and tell Matron that you've got your feet wet, and I have sent you to her because I think it better for you to go to bed at once in case you should catch a cold."

Alixe began to protest wildly at this, for so far she had done no preparation.

Her protests availed her nothing. Joey marched her off, delivered her over to Matron with the suggestion that it might be as well to take *all* due precautions, since both slippers and stockings were soaking wet, and left her to her fate.

And fate proved bitterly hard.

Alixe's mother was up at the Sonnalpe, where she was being kept under observation. Matron Venables knew this, having met pretty Frau von Elsen, and she was running no risks with Alixe. That young lady was ordered into a hot mustard bath, and when it was over, she was popped into a warm bed, her chest rubbed with camphorated oil, and a dose of nauseating cod liver oil added to complete the prevention. Finally, she was tucked up, and left, with strict orders not to put her arms out from under the blankets.

As for the others, Jo sent off all the practising people without more ado; made certain inquiries, which resulted in four more conspirators being condemned to copy out sundry poems in their best handwriting on Saturday evening (when the rest would be dancing and playing games); and wound up by treating them all to a lecture, which left them remarkably subdued for the time being.

"That's the worst of Jo!" sighed Enid Southern, as she and the rest were getting ready for bed that night. "She's always so on the spot! If we'd only known beforehand, we could have warned Alixe – Yes; I know you *did* have a shot, Hilda, but it didn't come to much, did it?

"Jo's a regular Johnny-on-the-spot," grumbled Mary Shaw. "*Anne* wouldn't have found it out – not so soon, anyway. Why was Jo taking prep? It was Anne's turn, and she ought to have been there."

"They were all doing extra science with Bill," said Dorothy Brentham. "Didn't you folk know?"

"Guess not. Alixe wouldn't have played the giddy goat if we *had*!"

What more they might have said about Jo will never be known, for at that moment Bill herself appeared to remind them that the silence bell had been rung five minutes ago, and to award a conduct mark to all those who had spoken after it had gone, which put a most effectual stop to any further conversation among them.

What Jo herself said in the privacy of the staff room, where she had been retelling the story of the evening's happenings for the benefit of the rest, was, "Middles don't improve a little bit. Goodness knows *we* were bad enough; but some of these imps beat us hollow!"

CHAPTER 13

Half Term Begins

Half term came at the beginning of November. The rain poured down early in the week, but cleared up later, though the weather remained cold and grey. As many as possible of the girls went home, but some had to stay at school, among them the Die Rosen people

On the Monday of that week, Joey Bettany made her way to the study to ring up her sister, and make inquiries about all the invalids. Mademoiselle was there, busy with her usual heavy mail, and she smiled sympathetically when the girl entered.

"You wish to telephone, my Jo?" she queried.

"If I may. You know, I could wring young Rix's neck for spoiling our half term like this," continued Rix's young aunt, as she lifted the receiver and began dialling the number. "There's poor Robin as well; *her* half term's spoilt – to say nothing of Stacie, and Daisy, and the Lintons. I haven't seen Robin since term began."

Mademoiselle smiled. "That is hard for you both. I must go, Joey. I will see you later, mon enfant."

"Yes, Mademoiselle – Oh, hello! Is that you, Madge? This is Jo."

Mademoiselle left the room, and Jo sat down to hear the last report of the Die Rosen family.

She rang off, and hung up the receiver, just as Mademoiselle re-entered the room. Mademoiselle had gone very thin, and there were shadows and dips in her face, which had lost its old, healthy colouring. She moved languidly, which was something new to Mademoiselle, who had always gone about her duties briskly, though she had never been of the bustling kind.

When she sat down, the girl went over and knelt down beside her. "Mademoiselle, aren't you fit *yet*?"

Mademoiselle looked down into the soft, black eyes lifted to hers. "Perhaps I am not so well yet, Joey. I do not grow younger, my child, and these attacks of malaise are trying."

"Are you worried about Miss Stewart?"

"Yes; I am a little. She has been quite ill, and the doctors tell me that she ought to attempt no more work this term. I have tried to persuade her to go home till after Christmas, but she refuses, as she fears lest her absence should make too much extra work for us."

Jo said nothing for a moment. Then: "But it needn't – or not much. If I stayed on till the end of term, her absence would really make very little difference, wouldn't it?" she asked slowly.

Mademoiselle looked at her. "I did not think you enjoyed teaching so much."

"Oh, it isn't that. But you've all been so good to me, I'd like to help you if I could – and Madge says it's no more than I *ought*," she added honestly. "If I stuck it till the end of term, don't you think you could tell Miss Stewart that we could manage all right; then she might go."

"It might just make the difference, Jo. I think if she knew that you were prepared to finish the term with us, she would consent. But are you prepared to do it? Remember, it will have to be for the whole five weeks left."

"I know; but I'd be a pig if I didn't after you've been

so jolly decent to me!" Jo was forgetting her grown-up dignity, and using schoolgirl speech in her earnestness. "Madge thinks so, too. We've just been discussing it, and she all but said I must. If you'll have me, I'm willing to have a shot, anyhow."

Mademoiselle put her arm round the girl, and drew her close and kissed her. "Thank you, Joey. It will be a great relief to me, and it will mean that as soon as Miss Stewart is fit to travel, we can send her home to rest and recuperate. Then, in all probability, she will be strong and well next term.

"Right you are! I'll do it," said Jo with decision.

"Thank you, ma chérie. And I have a plan for you, too. If Dr Jem will agree, how would you like to have the Robin here for half term? She could share your room, and you would be together for the whole weekend, which will be a long one. You see, we break up on Thursday this term and will not begin work again until the Wednesday morning, as Miss Stewart and I have both been on the sick list. Would you like it?"

"Oh, Mademoiselle! If she only could! Do you think Jem would agree? She's getting stronger every day, now; and she's been so well, ever since last year. Of course," Joey's face clouded a little, "if the rain comes again, he certainly *won't* agree."

"I will ring him up this afternoon and ask him," promised Mademoiselle. "Now, dear child, the bell is ringing for Prayers."

Jem, after Mademoiselle had explained the state of things to him, said that, provided the weather was good, there was no reason why the Robin should not come down for the holiday, and he undertook to manage Juliet Carrick, once a pupil of the Chalet School, and now Head

148

of the Annexe, so that she would agree to letting the little girl come down on the Thursday afternoon instead of waiting till the Friday morning, when the Annexe would begin its own half term.

"I'll tell her that Thursday suits me better than Friday," he said. "As it happens, it will. We have an important consultation on Friday, and I might be late in getting away. So the scaramouche is going to finish her term with you? Good for her!"

"Indeed, Jo is the dearest girl," said Mademoiselle quietly. "I only wish we might keep her here always. Her influence is excellent."

"Oh, come! That wouldn't do! We want Jo ourselves, you know. With all those babies in the nursery, Madge will need her sometimes."

"I know that. And I know she would not consent. But I cannot help wishing it."

"Aren't you feeling right again?" His voice came quickly. "Look here, Thérèse, I'm going to insist on a thorough overhaul when I bring the Robin down on Thursday. I'm inclined to think you need a change of medicine."

Mademoiselle would have protested, but he had guessed that and rang off on the final word. Though he had said nothing to her, he was beginning to think that there was something seriously wrong. The Head of the school sighed, and then laughed a little sadly before she went to seek Joey and tell her of the arrangements for half term.

Thursday came, a grey day, but quite fine. It was very cold, and the girls were thankful for their blazers. The stoves in the rooms were all glowing brightly, so that if it was cold out-of-doors, it was warm enough within.

Jo woke early, danced a noiseless fandango when she saw the weather, and then hurried into her clothes. When she was all ready to go downstairs, she turned to her table – since she had still half-an-hour left – and became very busy. The result of her work was a neat square parcel carefully tied up, and sealing-waxed within an inch of its life, which she later entrusted to Maria Marani, who was going home to Innsbruck, with certain instructions, and some money.

"You won't forget, and you *will* be careful, Maria, won't you?" she said.

Maria nodded, her little dark face glowing with eagerness, for Joey had entrusted her with an important secret. "I will be most careful, Jo, and indeed I know what to do, for I have been with Papa when he has registered his parcels."

"I don't know what it'll cost," continued Jo, "but if I haven't given you enough, ask your father to be a dear and let you have the rest, and I'll give it to you when you come back."

Maria laughed as she looked at the notes Joey had given her. "There is far more here than is needed, Jo. I shall have some to return to you when I come back."

"Indeed, you won't – get chocolates with it if there's any over. Yes, Maria; I mean it. I've plenty, goodness knows! I'm on an allowance now, you know, and so far I've spent next to nothing."

Maria gave way, and then ran off to put the precious parcel into her case before she locked it, while Joey went on to the staff room.

Over at St Clare's, the girls were thronging round the stove waiting for the gong to summon them to Frühstück.

"Oh, how cold it is;" shivered Polly, when she came down to the common room.

"It'll be colder than this," said Violet Allison, who was following her. "Wait till the snow comes! Then you really *will* find it cold."

"But so pretty," put in Stacie Benson, better again, and without the pinched look she had worn the previous week. "Jo always calls it 'Christmas-card Land' then."

"Does it snow much here?" asked Polly innocently.

A chorus of laughter greeted this. "Snow much! I just guess it *does*!" said Mary Shaw decisively. "You just wait!"

"Urrh! How horrid!" Polly shivered again. "I hate snow – all wet and messy! And then people walk about in it, and it turns to mud and looks horrid!"

"But no, Polly!" said Irma Ancokzky. "What can you mean? The snow is like powder. Then we play snowballs, and build forts to defend, and sledge and ski, and so many jolly things!"

Polly stared. "Is this true, or are you teasing me?" she asked doubtfully.

"But have you not heard of the winter sports in the Alps?" cried Irma.

"Yes; but that's Switzerland."

"And here, also. What mountains do you think ours are? There are winter sports at Innsbruck, and many people come from England for them. So it is here, only no one comes – "

"Except for the Carnival on the lake," put in Thelma Johansen. "The lake freezes, Polly, and people skate across instead of walking round. And in January, they light great bonfires round the lake on one day, and people come from all the villages round to skate and make merry –"

"Only we are not permitted to join in, for it is often rough," added Jeanne le Cadoulec.

"No; but we skate on our own when it's over," put in Kitty Burnett. "Jolly good fun, too!"

"Oh, you will love the snow here, Polly!" Irma assured her.

"I'll believe that when I see it," said Polly sceptically. "Anyway, it looks more like rain than snow at present."

"Oh, no! There aren't any clouds to speak of," said Kitty confidently. "I think it'll be fine today."

She proved to be right. The wind fell towards noon, and a queer hush prevailed. But no rain came, and no snow either. Fourteen hours saw all those who were going away for half term assembled in hall at Ste Thérèse's; and after the staff had seen that they were warmly wrapped up, and had everything they were likely to need, they said goodbye, and set off.

Miss Wilson and Miss Nalder took charge of one party, for they were spending the weekend at Innsbruck themselves. Miss Leslie and Matey had the people who were going to Salzburg or Kufstein. Matron Venables took charge of the few who were going up to the Sonnalpe.

All told, it was a big clearance, and, when the last had gone, the twenty-three girls left behind felt rather lost in the big buildings. They were to be at Ste Thérèse's though Miss Stewart would still stay in the sanatorium at St Clare's, with Nurse. They hoped that she would be well enough to travel by Thursday of the following week, when a doctor brother was coming to take her to her home in distant Herefordshire.

Miss Annersley would be in charge, and would have some help from Miss Norman and Miss Edwards, who had elected to stay behind this time. Little Mademoiselle

Lachenais was also to be at school, mainly to keep Mademoiselle Lepâttre company, for Dr Jem had ordained that she must remain in her own room and have nothing to do with the girls. He hoped that this rest would enable her to continue with her work till the end of term, when she hoped to go home to Paris. Mademoiselle Lachenais had at once declared that she would attend to her compatriot. But she now confided to Jo that when Mademoiselle did not require her, she meant to join the holiday party.

"Good!" said Jo. "We'll have a really good time this half term, even though we can't go to the Sonnalpe. I say, Mademoiselle! I've got an idea or two! We must have a pow-wow."

"A pow-wow?" Mademoiselle Lachenais looked puzzled. "What, then, is that?"

"A conference, if you like it better – I say! Is that voices I hear outside?"

Mademoiselle Lachenais glanced out of the window of the staff room, where they were. "Yes; it is our good Dr Jem and the Robin – but, *Joey!*"

For with a wild "Yoicks! Tally-ho!" Jo was out of her chair, and away downstairs to greet the little adopted sister she loved so dearly.

She reached the door just as the tall, fair doctor came to the step, his arm round the shoulders of the Robin. Joey wasted no time on him. With a hasty, "Hello, Jem! How are you?" she was at the Robin's side, clasping the child closely, and kissing her fondly.

"Oh, Robin, my Robin! How long it is since I've seen you!"

The Robin's arms were round her neck. "Joey – Joey! I have so longed for thee! It is six weeks – but *six weeks*

153

since I have seen thee!" In her excitement, she forgot her English, and lapsed into the tenderer French.

"Now, then, you two, when you've quite finished enacting the fond reunion scene, you'd better come in out of the cold," interrupted Dr Russell. "How are you, Joey? Teaching not too much for you? Not overdoing it, are you?"

Jo laughed, released the Robin, and lifted her face for his kiss. "Do I look like it? How's everyone at Die Rosen? Oh, Jem, you don't know how I'm longing to get back to you all! I've never been homesick in my life, but I've come uncommonly near it this term."

"Yes; it's been a trying time all round," he agreed, as he drew them into the house and shut the door. "However, we seem to be getting to the end of it at last, thank goodness! The measles cases are all out of quarantine, except David, who finishes the day after tomorrow. Rix is much better, too, though he still whoops on occasion."

"And the babies?"

"Growing at great speed! You'll see them as soon as it's safe for you to come up. Jackie's a big boy now – got seven teeth, and very fit and bonny. Sybil will be crawling all over before long. And Primula Mary has kept well, and is much stronger."

Jo nodded her satisfaction at this last statement. Primula Mary, Mrs Venables' youngest child, had been almost tragically frail when she had been brought to the mountains in the early summer, and there had been real reason to fear for her. Evidently she was responding well to the sparkling mountain air and the strict régime her doctor uncle was using for her.

"Mademoiselle is in the study," was all she said. "You go to her while I take the Robin to get her things off. The house is warm, and she oughtn't to stay bundled up like this in it."

"Quite right," he said, as he turned aside to the study. "Here's her case, Joey. See that she puts on her blazer when she's untied."

Joey took the small suitcase, and led the Robin away, while he went into the study to see the Head.

"Is everyone here, at Ste Thérèse's?" asked the Robin, as she hung up her brown beret on a peg and let Joey unbutton her coat.

"Everyone who is staying. The rest went off well over an hour ago. Let me look at you, mein Blümchen. What rosy cheeks! You look as if life at the Annexe agreed with you!"

"It *is* fun. But I would rather be here with you," said the Robin, as she wriggled into her blazer, and then stood back to let Joey look at her.

"Not growing very much yet, are you," said Jo, surveying the small, slim person before her. "You're not going to take after Uncle Ted in that respect, anyhow. And you've still got your pretty curls, thank goodness! I was terrified lest Madge would let them grow long. I suppose you must, some day. But we'll wait for it, I hope. You wouldn't be the same with long hair."

The Robin chuckled. "But you are growing yours, Joey. How neat it looks! How do you do it?"

Jo turned solemnly round to let her see and admire the neat arrangement of clasps and pins that kept her long-short locks tidy. "This is only till it's long enough to wear in ear-phones. But the ends will stick out when I do it that way, do what I will. It touches my shoulders now, though, and I'm hoping that by Easter, at least, I'll be able to plait it."

"Won't it be funny – to see you with tidy hair!" The Robin gave a gurgle.

"Don't be impertinent, you monkey! Come along now; Mademoiselle will want to see you before we go to the others."

Hand in hand they went to the study, where they found Mademoiselle and Dr Jem chatting together. The Head kissed and petted the Robin for a minute or two, and then released her, saying, "Take her to the others, my Jo. You must bring her up to see me every morning while she stays, for your so-strict brother tells me I must not be with you girls at all this weekend."

"Certainly not," said the doctor. "You are to have a complete rest, Thérèse, or you'll never last the term out."

The Robin obediently kissed Mademoiselle, and went off with Joey to the common room, where the twenty-three girls left behind were all seated round the tables or at the windows, busy with various amusements.

There were shouts of welcome when the pair appeared, for most of the girls knew the Robin, who had been at the Chalet School before the Annexe had been opened, and had been everybody's darling.

Amy Stevens, Margia's younger sister, had been at the Annexe until this term, when she had been pronounced strong enough to return to the larger school, and she and the Robin were great chums, though there was more than two years between them in age. They met joyfully, and presently were seated together on the floor over a big jigsaw which Amy had been trying to complete, while the rest of the girls returned to their own interests.

Seeing that the Robin was happily occupied, Joey glanced round, and then crossed the room to the wide window seat where Polly Heriot was curled up by herself, looking out at the grey lake and sky.

"What on earth are you looking at?" she asked curiously. "It's appallingly bleak out there, and there's nothing to see. Thank goodness we shall have lights presently! This grey monotony gives me the jim-jams!"

"I was only wondering if it would snow soon," explained Polly, moving in order to make room for her. "I'm dying to see it! Irma was telling me all sorts of fairy-tales about it being like dust."

Jo shouted. "What a simile! I'm surprised at Irma! Oh, it's powdery, all right, and absolutely dry. But to liken anything so sparkling and lovely as snow to *dust* . . . " Words apparently failed her at this point, and Polly laughed.

"Well, anyhow, they all say it just brushes off you, and doesn't wet you. *I've* never seen any snow like that," observed the doubting Thomas. "I'm looking to see if it's likely to come. It'll be something out of the common when it does, if all their yarns are true! What do you think, Joey? Will it be along soon?"

Joey peered out into the gathering gloom. "It doesn't look impossible," she conceded. "In fact, it wouldn't surprise me in the least if it snowed before midnight. I don't think it's likely to come much before then, though. You come along and meet the Robin, Polly. The snow won't come any sooner for you sitting there, trying to mesmerize it!"

This was true, besides being sensible, so Polly left her post at the window, where she had been beginning to feel a little chilly, and went with Joey to meet the Robin. Both of them were bidden sit down and help, for the puzzle contained eight hundred pieces, and the two little girls

157

were beginning to be afraid that it was beyond them.

The only breaks came when Joey and the Robin were called to bid the doctor goodbye when he left, and Kaffee und Kuchen. Otherwise, they continued with their pleasing occupation until Abendessen came, and after Abendessen it was the Robin's bedtime, for, even at half term, there might be no slackening of the régime under which she was being brought up. Her pretty Polish mother had died of tuberculosis, and, along with that mother's dark beauty, the Robin had inherited her fragile constitution. So early hours, plenty of milk and fresh air, and very little excitement were hers.

When Joey called her, she went off blithely, full of glee because she was to sleep with her adored "big sister", who attended to all the details of her toilet, heard her prayers, and then tucked her up in the small bed set beside her own.

"Gute Nacht, mein Engelkind," she said, bending to kiss the rosy face. "Your guardian angel watch over you all night long!"

"Good night, Joey, *dearest* Joey!" said the Robin, with a hug.

Jo tucked in the blankets more securely, and then went to the window to make sure that the draught-board was in. As she opened the curtains she uttered an exclamation.

"What is it, Joey?" asked the Robin sleepily.

"Snow, Robinette! It's coming down in cart-loads! With any luck we shall get a snow fight tomorrow, to say nothing of other joys! Now you go to sleep, mein Blümchen. I'll be coming presently. I know Miss Annersley means us all to get to bed in decent time tonight. Schlaf' wohl!" And with a final kiss, Jo went off downstairs to announce the joyful news that the snow had come.

CHAPTER 14

A "Different" Party

Excitement had made the girls drowsy, and it was nearly eight o'clock before they woke the next morning. As there were so few of them, they were sleeping in four dormitories. Polly, Suzanne Mercier, Biddy O'Ryan, Kitty Burnett, Stacie Benson and Dorothy Brentham had been put into the Yellow Dormitory, along with Cornelia Flower and Margia Stevens, who slept there normally; Cornelia and Margia had their own cubicles, and the others were distributed round the dormitory.

"What's the weather doing?" demanded Margia from her cubicle near the door as she sat up with a shiver. "Urrh! Isn't it cold?"

There was the sound of clothes being thrown back, and then a bump told that Cornelia was out of bed and pulling back the window-curtain. She uttered a cry of surprise.

"Say, girls! It's snowing – snowing fit to beat the band! Just come and look!"

Rules were always more or less in abeyance during half term, so there was a rush to the two window cubicles. Margia, in her hurry, contrived to trip over Biddy O'Ryan, and the pair of them came down with a crash, Biddy giving vent to a howl as she went.

"Ow, Margia Stevens! 'Tis yourself's the heavy gerrl! Be getting off me hair, will yez, now?"

Margia picked herself up in a hurry. "Well, I haven't killed you," she said soothingly. "Shut up, Biddy!

159

You'll disturb Mademoiselle if you squall like that! Get up, now, and don't lie there howling like a banshee! – O-oh! I *say!*" For by this time she was in Cornelia's cubicle, and gazing out of the window at the falling snow, which was coming down as if it never meant to leave off.

"Just into November and the snows have come! Oh, well; it's no earlier than last year, after all."

"It's come earlier than this before now," remarked Cornelia, as she turned to find her dressing gown.

"But – but isn't it *awful*?" gasped Polly from the other cubicle. "I never even imagined snow like this! I wouldn't like to be out in it!"

"Nor should I," said Dorothy Brentham, with a shake of her head of yellow curls.

"I *have* been out when it was as bad as this," said Margia, beginning to stroll back to her own abode. "D'you remember, Corney?"

Cornelia, who had left the window and was now hunting for her stockings beneath the bed, replied in a muffled voice, "No; I don't. When was it?"

"Corney! Of course you do! Don't you remember that first term the Saints came here?"

"Who are the Saints?" demanded Polly.

"Oh, goodness! Don't you know that yet? It's St Scholastika's, at the other side of the lake. They came two years ago, and we did *not* love them at first."

"Jolly good reason why," said Cornelia, wriggling out from beneath the bed. "Here, you folk, vamoose! I want to get dressed, and I guess you'd better be thinking about it yourselves. It must be mighty late if the light's anything to go by."

They went, reluctantly, and when everyone was busy,

Polly lifted up her voice again. "Why didn't you like the Saints, Margia?"

"Oh, we just didn't fit in," said Margia hurriedly. "We had one or two rows; but it all came right in the end. They'e jolly decent, really. But don't you remember, Corney, that morning when Maynie had the Seniors, and Charlie us Middles, and we went for a walk, and got caught coming back? I believe the Seniors got it worse than we did, for they weren't anywhere near home when it came on. But I had quite enough of it as it was. It was a few days before we took that walk when the lake path gave way, and we all had to climb up to Mechthau and go over the shoulder of the mountain and down the Pass to get home. *Now* do you remember?"

Cornelia did. "Guess I do. That awful ass Elaine Gilling rowed with Mary," she said reminiscently. "And that other creature, Vera Smithers, was there. Yes; it was some storm."

"As bad as this – really?" asked Polly, pausing in the act of pulling on a stocking.

"Every bit – if not worse," said Margia promptly. "You don't know what it's like when it starts to snow here. You wait till the end of this term. You'll know all about it then."

Polly thought she knew a little already after seeing that mad dervish-dance of snowflakes outside. However, she said no more, but went on with her dressing. When the bell rang, they all raced downstairs in a hurry.

"We must have wasted a fearful lot of time at the window," said Margia to Cornelia. "I didn't think we were standing there so long. Did you, Corney?"

Cornelia shook her head. "Guess 'twas longer than we thought," she said.

161

Suzanne Mercier was in advance of them, and while they were only just at the foot of the stairs, she had gone on, and into the common room. Now they heard her exclaim, "Mon Dieu! Que'est-se qu'il y a?"

At once they tore after her, to find her gazing at a huge sheet of drawing paper which covered the notice board. It had a border of rabbits in various attitudes – Mademoiselle Lachenais was very clever at sketching animals – and inside the border was written:

INVITATION

The pleasure of the company of all girls left at school for half term is requested tonight at

A GRAND SHEETS-AND-PILLOWCASE PARTY

AMUSEMENTS AND RECREATION!

COMPETITIONS! DANCING! SINGSONG!

R.S.V.P. to members of the staff room.

Those present read this striking notice, and then turned and looked at each other. Margia was the first to speak.

"What," she demanded of the assembled circle, "*is* a sheets-and-pillowcase party?"

"Is it zat we have to bring our sheets and pillowcases wiz us?" suggested Suzanne, who, despite several years at an English school, had never yet mastered the English "th".

"Yes; but what on earth do we *do* with them?" asked Cornelia, still staring at the invitation.

Dorothy Brentham, who had now joined the group, had a suggestion to make: "P'raps we're going to make up beds on the floor like a kind of camp – "

"It says 'dancing'," Cornelia reminded her. "Oh, here's Thora! P'raps *she* knows! – Grüss Gott, Thora! Come and see this, and tell us what you think it means."

The big Norwegian returned Cornelia's greeting with a laughing "Grüss Gott!" and then came to the notice board, and read the notice it bore.

"What on earth is a sheets-and-pillowcase party?" asked Cornelia. "D'you know, Thora?"

Thora shook her head. "I never heard of one before. I cannot think what it can be. It is Jo's idea, of course. Our best plan is to catch her, and ask what it means."

Polly Heriot skipped out of the room on the word to seek Jo, and met her just outside the door, the Robin clinging to her arm, and looking up at her with merry laughter. Polly eagerly grabbed Jo's free arm, and exclaimed, "Jo! Do come and tell us what a sheets-and-pillowcase party is, for we've no idea!"

Jo grinned. "Haven't you? How fearfully dull you must all be! All right; I'm coming – In you go, Robinette, and don't get into any draughts, whatever you do."

The Robin chuckled as she danced into the room, to be seized on by Amy Stevens, and borne off to the notice board to inspect the cause of all the excitement. Jo was promptly besieged by the rest, all demanding to know what it meant.

"Guess you're the one to do the explaining," said Cornelia. "It's your stunt – I know that all right."

"Clever child!" said Jo aggravatingly.

"What's it mean, Jo?" asked Margia, pushing back the thick curls that were always tumbling into her eyes.

163

"Exactly what it says, my child." Then Jo condescended to explain. "You manufacture some sort of fancy costume from two sheets and a pillowcase, and there are prizes for costumes. You've got all day to do it in, and there certainly won't be any going out while this storm lasts, so it'll occupy your time nicely. There goes the gong for Frühstück, and if you're all as hungry as I am, you're not sorry. Come along, all of you. And when it's over, don't forget to R.S.V.P. to the invite!" And Jo walked off to the Speisesaal, chuckling to herself over their stunned faces.

The imperative sound of the gong sent them after her, but for once there was little conversation at Frühstück. Everyone was much too busy wondering what sort of a costume she could evolve from two sheets and a pillowcase to want to talk. Some of the very tinies were thoroughly perplexed, but Miss Edwards and Miss Norman, their own special mistresses, who were also spending the weekend at the school though they were not on duty, promised to help them.

"Can we *cut* the sheets?" asked Cornelia suddenly, between two mouthfuls of roll and jam.

"*Cut* your sheets, Cornelia? Most certainly *not*!" cried Miss Annersley. "Please, all of you, understand once and for all that your sheets and pillowcases are to remain intact. You may safety-pin them, or stitch them lightly; but there is to be no cutting."

There was silence again after this, and when grace had been said, they all went off to make their beds and tidy their cubicles, still exercising their brains to find costumes that could be made of sheets and pillowcases without cutting the materials.

"But I say!" exclaimed Dorothy Brentham suddenly,

164

"if we're going to use them for dresses, what's the use of making our beds now?"

"You're all going to have clean ones for the dresses, of course," said Matron Gould, appearing at that moment laden with sheets, while Jo followed with pillowcases. "Here you are – two each, and one pillowcase. If you want any more, you must come and ask me. I shall be in the linen room from ten till eleven in case anyone should require another. Now get on with your work as quickly as possible."

She left them to go on to the next dormitory, and they hurried to finish their beds and tidying. Once that was ended, they all departed to the common room to discuss dresses, and there the staff found them when they came in for Prayers.

Prayers over, the girls gathered round the mistresses for a few minutes, talking eagerly.

"Mademoiselle," cried Cornelia, "are you folks going to dress up too?"

"Mais certainement," replied Mademoiselle, laughing. "Is it that you wish to keep all the fun to yourselves?"

"Listen, you people," said Miss Annersley, "We are offering prizes for the prettiest costume, for the most outstanding costume, and for the funniest. Now we are going to leave you to it. We have our own dresses to make. Come along, everybody!" And she swept off her colleagues, while the girls were still gasping.

"Well!" cried Cornelia, the ever-ready, as the door closed on the staff, "I guess this is going to need some right smart thinking. I'm off to the Fifth to think it out by myself. So long, everybody!"

Most of the elder girls followed her example, and Jo Bettany, sitting in the library sewing, with the Robin beside her, was startled when the door was opened, and Margia Stevens, accompanied by her young sister, came in with a hunted expression, which changed to one of disgust as she saw the room already occupied.

"You here!" she exclaimed. "There simply isn't a solitary place in the house where you can be decently alone!"

"Sorry I can't go to my own room," said Jo amiably. "It's too near Mademoiselle. And besides that, something's gone wrong with the stove, and till Eitel can put it right, Matron says it's much too cold for me. Besides, Robin couldn't sit there, and I've got her dress to do, as well as my own. Why don't you try Vater Bär's music room?"

"Good idea! So I will. Come on, Amy!" And Margia vanished.

It continued to snow throughout the day, the snow whirling down so dizzily that it was impossible to catch even a glimpse of the lake, which lay barely four feet beyond the palisade. Ordinarily, those in charge might have found it difficult to keep the girls amused. But thanks to the latest idea for a party, nobody even asked for amusement.

"When does the party begin?" asked Yvette Mercier of Miss Annersley during Mittagessen.

The senior mistress looked at Jo. "Didn't you put the time on the invitation, Jo?"

"Mercy! I believe I forgot all about it!" cried Jo. "Sorry, everyone, I'll go and rectify that as soon as I've finished."

She finished her Kalbsbraten (stuffed roast veal), and then asked permission to go to the common room for a few minutes. Miss Annersley nodded her head and laughed, and Jo fled to enter the hours of the party, returning to find the others busy with Apfeltorte.

"All serene," she said, as she took her seat again. "You'll all see when you're finished."

They swarmed round the board as soon as they were freed, to find that the party would take place from nineteen to twenty-two hours, whereat some of the smaller folk clapped their hands. Late hours were almost unknown at the Chalet School.

"What about Abendessen?" demanded Margia of Jo, who had elected to desert the staff.

"Not till twenty hours," returned Jo. "It's part of the party – sorry, everyone! That was not meant for a pun!"

"Thank goodness!" Margia heaved a sigh of relief. "Then I may be able to finish in time!"

"I *have* finished," said Cornelia with a self-satisfied smirk.

"Corney Flower! You *haven't*!"

"'Have, though. I finished early this afternoon, and I've been reading for ages."

"Then you must be nothing but safety pins."

"It's sewn – every bit of it," said Cornelia indignantly.

"The age of miracles is still with us," said Jo lazily. "Corney Flower has made a frock in about three hours, and hasn't safety-pinned it! Better send the news to the daily papers!"

"What about your own?" demanded Stacie. "I don't see where you've got time to make yours, for you've been busy with Robin and me all day. What are you going to do?"

"Aha! That, as Hamlet so neatly says, is the question. Wait and see, my child."

"What are you being, Polly?" asked Jo, as she handed her cup to Thora.

Polly chuckled, "I'll give you your own answer: wait and see."

"Impertinent infant! I ought to rise and ker*rush* you, but I can't be bothered. Lights ho, someone! I can't see the way to my own mouth!"

Dorothy Brentham obligingly rose to the situation, and the much-needed lights were switched on. Polly and Yvette ran to draw the curtains, and the big room took on an air of cosy comfort.

"That's better!" sighed Jo. "Thanks, Thora. Well, if you'll all excuse me, I'll go and finish. Coming, Robin?"

"But yes, Joey!" The Robin jumped up from her stool, and the pair left the room. Margia, who still had a good deal to do at her own costume, though Amy's was finished, ran off, too. One by one the others followed, and when Miss Annersley presently peeped in, the room was empty. She nodded to someone behind the door, and beckoned.

"All right; they've gone! Come along, Jeanne, and you other four! It's no use hoping for Joey's help. She declares that she means to be a girl for the weekend. Bring those draperies, Ivy, and you fetch that screen, Dorothy."

Miss Norman appeared, laden with crimson curtains, and Miss Edwards followed her, dragging a tall screen after her. Mademoiselle Lachenais and Matron Gould came last, bearing between them a table which was covered with sundry parcels.

"Where shall we put it, Hilda?" asked the latter anxiously.

Miss Annersley looked round. "In that corner, I think," she said, gesticulating. "We'll set the screen before it, and hang up a notice to keep the girls off."

They bore the table to the corner, and Miss Edwards staggered after them with her screen, while Miss Norman, having dropped her draperies on a nearby settee, hurried from the room, to return with one of the maids helping her to carry a tall library ladder.

The staff then became busy. They tacked up the curtains round the wall, and draped against them long paper chains and sprays of artificial flowers. Miss Norman took off the ordinary light-shades, and substituted home-made ones of crimson paper. The furniture was all set back against the wall, and the rugs were rolled up and carried off to the nearest form room. When at length the work was completed, the common room had been transformed.

"Most effective!" said Miss Edwards, when it was all done.

"Most," agreed Matron Gould. "But do you know the time?"

They glanced hastily at their watches, and then fled with little shrieks of horror, for they had barely twenty minutes in which to change and be ready to welcome their guests.

They were all in time, all looking very festive in their unwonted attire. Miss Annersley was garbed as a Roman matron, with her hair banded with white tape. Matron Gould, who stood five feet ten in her stockings, had elected to appear as an arch-druid, with a Welsh harp slung across her shoulders. Miss Norman was a Scots fisher-lass, with upturned skirt, and the pillowcase folded and tied under her chin. Miss Edwards was a geisha, and as she was very small and dark, she looked very well.

But Mademoiselle Lachenais had outdone them all, for she was attired as a Normandy peasant, with the pillowcase turned into a charming cap, pleated and wired to make it stand up. Her vivacious little dark face stood the dead white admirably, and Miss Norman cried, "Why, Jeanne, I'd no idea you were so pretty!" which brought a most becoming blush to Mademoiselle's cheeks.

The next moment, there was a tap at the door, and their first guests appeared – Thora, Margia, and Amy. Thora had transformed herself into a Norwegian peasant girl; Amy was a white butterfly, with wings made of sheets of tissue-paper, wired to the right shape; Margia herself wore flowing robes, a wreath of white-paper leaves round her brown curls, and a sheet of paper in one hand, on which was inscribed "The Republic."

"Plato!" gasped Miss Annersley. "Well, upon my word!"

"Not bad, is it?" said Margia complacently. "Who's this coming?"

A ballet dancer, her skirts held out by means of canes and wire, tripped in, accompanied by a nun, who was already complaining that she felt as if she were being boiled alive. Then others appeared, and great had been the ingenuity the girls showed. Suddenly, there was a loud hooting outside, and an abnormally tall figure rushed on them, waving batlike wings. One or two of the little ones shrieked, and rushed to hide their faces in the nearest big person. But Margia recognized the movements of the ghost which had swooped down on them, and cried out, "Corney Flower! I know it is!"

The next moment, they were thronging round her, demanding to know how she had managed it. For reply, the figure squirmed a minute, an opening appeared somewhere about the middle of the lengthy figure, and Cornelia's square-jawed face with twinkling blue eyes grinned out at them.

"How have you done it?" demanded Margia.

"Hockey-stick strapped to my back and head. My wings? Oh, badminton racquets, of course. It's a bit confining, but I guess I can stand it for an hour or so."

"We shall all be ready to change by that time," sighed the nun. "I feel as if I were cooked already!"

"Here come Joe and Stacie and the Robin," said her sister Suzanne. "They are the last, so we can now begin."

All eyes were turned to the door, through which a tall Indian lady in white sari appeared, followed by an Arab chieftain, and an angel with great curving wings, sandalled feet, and glistening silver halo laid on the thick black curls. The Robin looked a picture, as everyone agreed, and the other two were quite effective. Jo had "scrounged" all the bangles and bead-strings she could, and the result was that whenever she moved, she jingled musically.

"'Tis a nose-ring you ought to have," said Biddy O'Ryan.

"Not likely!" retorted Jo, "I've got ear-rings – Mademoiselle lent me a pair – and the screws hurt, but I'm so afraid of losing them, I daren't slacken them."

"You'll soon get accustomed to them," said Miss Norman soothingly. "The first dance is a waltz. Will you have it with me, Joey? Matron is going to play."

The arch-druid sat down at the piano, and the floor was soon filled with merry girls, as the lilting notes of Strauss's "Morgenblätter" went rippling through the room. The angel, the butterfly and the ghost found it somewhat difficult – wings and a hockey-stick are not the best adornments when dancing – but they managed, and enjoyed themselves enormously.

Abendessen found them all thankful to cast aside their trappings and change into the ordinary brown velvet frocks of evening wear. The prizes had already been allotted, Miss Annersley told them, and they would be more comfortable in their usual garb. They raced off upstairs, and changed hurriedly, and were soon down again, consuming sandwiches, jellies, creams, fruits, sweets, lemonade, and coffee, as if they hadn't had a meal all day.

"Where are Joey and the Robin?" asked Mademoiselle Lachenais, suddenly pausing in the act of helping Amy Stevens to lemon sponge.

Everyone looked round. Neither was to be seen.

"Joey must have sewn herself or the Robin into the dress, and is having to cut free," suggested Margia.

It seemed the likeliest solution of the problem, and would have been accepted; but at that moment Joey herself appeared at the door of the Speisesaal, desperation in her face.

"Matron!" she said. "For goodness' sake come and help me! The enamel on the Robin's halo can't have been quite dry. The heat must have melted it a little, and now it's stuck."

"*What*?" exclaimed Matron, while the rest sat, stunned to silence by this happening.

"I can't get it off," repeated Joey. "I've tried and tried, but I can't move it without pulling her hair out by the roots. For pity's sake, come and see what *you* can do!"

With an indescribable expression, Matron got to her feet and followed the agitated Jo from the room. Just as she shut the door, Cornelia's clarion tones could be heard pronouncing on the catastrophe: "Gee! Well, I guess at that rate they'll have to *shave* the Robin to get rid of it! – Miss Annersley, what will they do till they can get her a wig?"

Do what she would, Matron could not get that obstinate halo removed from the Robin's head. It stuck firmly, and gave way before neither hot water, turpentine, nor anything else she could suggest.

172

"There's no help for it; we must cut it away," she said at length, when the Robin had been reduced to tears, and Jo was in the depths of despair. "What possessed you to use enamel at all, Jo, I can't think! Now don't cry, Robin. I'll get my embroidery scissors, and cut as carefully as I can. Miss Annersley will keep back some supper for us, so you won't miss anything but a little dancing. Stay with her, Jo, while I get the scissors."

The Robin obediently choked back her tears, and Jo, looking like the tragic muse, stayed with her. Matron returned in a few minutes with her scissors, and was as good as her word. With the greatest care, she snipped at the obstinate curls, and at length the poor little angel was free from her halo without much damage.

"Now come and wash your face," said Matron. "You certainly can't go to take the first prize for the prettiest dress looking like that!"

"Have I won that?" asked the Robin doubtfully.

"Yes; yours was by far the prettiest. We decided on it at once," said kind Matron.

The Robin cheered up. "I didn't expect that. Joey, do you hear? Is it not nice?"

Joey's face cleared. "Ever so nice, my Robin."

"And who has won the others?" asked the Robin, as they went to the bathroom.

"You'll see when you've had your supper," said Matron. "Make haste, both of you."

Jo hastily washed her hands, and then pinned up her straying locks, by which time the Robin looked her usual self, though her top curls had gone. Indeed, when they got downstairs to the Speisesaal, Amy Stevens voiced the views of the others when she said, "Why, you look just the same!"

"What did you expect?" demanded Jo.

Amy giggled. "Corney said Robin would have to be shaved and wear a wig," she said.

"Corney's got a lurid imagination," commented Matron, as she sat down to her jelly. "All we had to do was to cut the hair round the edge of the halo. Now run along, all of you, and leave us to get our supper."

The girls trooped off to the common room to dance again, and the three left went on with their meal.

"All the same, it was a senseless thing to do, Jo, and I can't think why you did it," said Miss Annersley. "You might have known that the enamel would stick."

"It said on the tin it was quick-drying," protested Jo. "It said it would harden in two hours, and I did the halo before Mittagessen to give it a chance."

"I can't help what it said. You've seen the result for yourself," said Miss Annersley severely. "I do wish you'd try to grow up now!"

"Oh, Miss Annersley! Don't *you* rub it in! I feel aged as it is," said Jo with a sigh.

Miss Annersley smiled. "A sure sign of how young you really are. Well, it's over now. Hurry up with your supper, and then we'll present the prizes."

"How did you come to have them?" asked Jo.

"Miss Edwards went down to Innsbruck this morning," said Miss Annersley.

"In all that snow?"

"Eigen took her. He knows every inch of the way."

"Oh, I see. How nice of her to go!"

Miss Annersley left them after that, and when they finally reached the common room, dancing was still going on. Miss Norman clapped her hands when she saw them, the music stopped, and everyone looked round.

"Prizes, now! said Miss Annersley. "Sit down, all of you."

Miss Norman and Miss Edwards carried the table from behind the screen, and set it in the middle of the floor. The senior mistress took up her position behind it, and Mademoiselle Lachenais read out the list. The Robin won first prize for the prettiest dress, and Polly, as a skating girl, received second. The most original went to Margia Stevens, and Suzanne Mercier. Cornelia won the funniest, with Biddy O'Ryan (as a snowball) the second. Then came a surprise.

"Most applicable, Yvette Mercier, and Thora Helgersen," read Mademoiselle Lachenais.

The ex-nun came up blushing and delighted to receive the fountain pen she had won; and big Thora was delighted, too, with her little brooch. The four "babies" had boxes of sweets, and Jo got a book she had long coveted for being "most helpful".

"Oh, I'm glad you've got something, Joey," said Stacie Benson when it was over, and the girls were dancing again. "You practically made the dresses for Robin and me, and you hadn't any time left for yourself."

"I'm glad to get this," said Jo, with a pat for André Maurois' latest novel. "But it was a surprise. That Indian get-up couldn't have won me anything. You couldn't have anything much simpler."

"That's just what I'm saying," said Stacie. "You gave all your time and ideas to us. It's only fair you should have something."

"Oh, rats!" said Jo hastily. "Hello – Subject and Object? Good! Come along!" And she led the way to the circle they were forming, while Matron took the sleepy Juniors off to bed.

She returned half-an-hour later to find the entire party arguing as to whether Cyrano de Bergerac had had a handkerchief or not, this having been Jo's idea when she and Polly had gone out. Jo, who was the Object, had stoutly maintained that she was vegetable, and many and varied had been the guesses, till at length they had had to give it up. She had then proclaimed what she was, and stuck to it, saying, that, as in those days there was no artificial silk, it must be linen, and that was a vegetable all right.

Miss Norman vowed that Cyrano would certainly never have such a thing, and the camp was divided. Asked for her opinion, Matron declared that she knew nothing about the gentleman, whereupon at least six people tried to enlighten her at once, in the midst of which the clock struck the hour, and Miss Annersley promptly put an end to the babel by ruling that the party was over.

CHAPTER 15

Statues – and a Sequel

Next morning, they woke to find the storm at an end for the time being, and the land covered with great drifts of white snow, while the clear, grey-blue sky promised a fine day.

Polly, gazing out at it from the common room window, heaved a sigh of delight, "I never even imagined snow could look so lovely! D'you think they'll let us go out in it?"

"I expect so," said Stacie Benson, joining her. "It wants frost, though, to make it right for walking. We shouldn't get far in this!"

"Why not?"

"It's so powdery, we should sink at once. And some of those drifts would be above our heads if we went through them," said Stacie thoughtfully.

However, when bedroom work was finished, they were all told to put on their winter clothes, for they were to go out for a couple of hours.

"No chance of a walk," said Miss Annersley. "We don't want to have to dig you out of the drifts. But Eitel has swept some paths for you, and it is going to freeze, so you can run along. Only keep moving."

Thrilling over the novelty of it, Polly got into climbing breeches, nailed boots, pullover, leather jacket that zipped up to her chin, and crossed-over woollen shawl. She wriggled her head into a close-fitting cap that covered her ears, and her hands into mitts, and was ready. There was no sun, and the sky gave no signs of its coming, so the girls were not expected to wear snowglasses.

"But if the sun *should* come, then you must all fly," said Miss Annersley. "We don't want any cases of snow-blindness."

"What's that?" asked Polly of Jo, as they went along the passage.

"Horrid!" said Jo, who had had a taste of it. "Everything goes red and swimmy. So mind you scoot if the sun does come."

Outside, the girls found themselves walking between walls of snow that were well over the heads of all but the tallest. However, it was outside, and that was all that mattered. They ran races, tossed snowballs, and generally enjoyed themselves. Then Jo had an inspiration.

"Let's make figures in snow," she proposed.

"Snowmen?" shrieked Amy and the Robin. "Oh, yes!"

"As it happens, I didn't mean anything so common-place," said Jo with dignity. "We'll choose some sort of statue and try to make it. If we pack the snow hard and then cut it out, we ought to be able to manage all right."

The noise they made over this brilliant idea brought the staff out to see who was being murdered, and they joined in at once.

"Let's make up groups of so many, and each take one statue and see who can do best," proposed Miss Norman.

No sooner said than done. Four groups of the girls and one of the staff set to work at once. First they built up huge piles of snow, pressing it down to make it more solid. All the shovels in the toolhouse and the kitchens were commandeered; and Jo, unable to get one of these useful implements, went off with the biggest bowl she could find, despite the protests made by Maria, the Ste Thérèse's cook.

"We'd better not try to make arms sticking out, I suppose?" said Thora doubtfully. "The snow does not stick well, and they would drop off, I am afraid."

"I'd advise lying-down positions," said Miss Edwards, pausing in her task of flattening the snow her colleagues brought her.

"We're going to do an upright one," said Jo. "We needn't have arms flying all over the place."

"*We're* doing Plato," said Margia, with an air. "Ought he to have a book, Joey?"

"Talk sense! You know quite well they only had scrolls in those days. If that's all you know, I'd advise you to choose something you *do* know," said Jo, staggering under the heaped-up dish she held.

Margia sniffed. "And I'd advise *you* to leave most of the modelling to the others. I'm sure Herr Laubach would say so."

There was a roar of laughter at this. Herr Laubach and Joey had had many a passage of arms, for drawing was decidedly *not* her gift. The finale had come about a year before, when she had set out to see how trying she could be, and he, losing his temper, had flung paper, pencils and rubber at her head. As a result, Jo had been removed from all art classes and put on to extra maths, for it was felt that the irritable art master must be protected against any further loss of dignity. As Jo hated maths, she got only what she deserved, as everyone had rubbed well in, so she flushed now, but said nothing further.

At length, everyone decided that the snow piles were large enough to begin modelling. And very tantalizing they

179

found it. Just as you got a really classical nose shaped, it either sank in the middle, or the end turned snub, or it fell off altogether. Those who had not been wise enough to keep to simple lines, soon found their mistake. Arms were worse than noses, and hands were simply dreadful.

At Jo's suggestion, her group had made a statue of little Ste Thérèse of Lisieux, with her hands folded on her breast. The severe lines of the Carmelite habit were much easier than a Greek chiton, for they fell to the feet.

Margia's group had also managed quite well with Plato's flowing robes. But his beard had been simply dreadful, and the scroll had had to be given up. Nor was his profile Greek, for his nose was a decided pug!

Thora's six had a pretty representation of Flora, and had been sensible enough to portray her lying among flowers. It is true Jo asked what "those funny-looking lumps of snow about her are?" But at least none of her head dropped away.

Cornelia, nothing if not ambitious, had aimed at the Statue of Liberty, and the less said the better about the maledictions uttered against the lady as they struggled with her torch and her rays of light. In the end, they had to leave out these important parts, and then, as Yvette pointed out, she might have been anything.

The staff had produced a young knight asleep with his hands clasping his sword. They had meant to give him a helmet, but no one could decide how the helmet should go, so they left it off, and gave him a deep fringe instead. The girls cheered this loudly, and the staff felt rewarded for their hard work.

By this time, it was time for Mittagessen, and they all went in with glowing cheeks and tremendous appetites. They had intended going out after the meal, and snow-balling the statues; but when Miss Annersley poked a head out to see what it was like, she found a decided change had taken place. The air was bitter, and it was plain that it was freezing hard. The girls had had a strenuous morning, and some of them were looking sleepy. Besides, yellowish clouds were beginning to float across the horizon, sure harbingers of more snow. So she told them they must remain indoors for the rest of the day, and they settled down contentedly enough with books, letters, jigsaws, sewing, painting – and always chatter. No one thought any more about those somewhat ghostly figures left to freeze solid.

Meanwhile, the cold intensified, and the statues grew harder. When Jo went to draw the curtains before Kaffee und Kuchen, she gave an exclamation of delight, for the snowy scene was glittering and sparkling under the warm light flowing from the windows, and the whole landscape looked as if it were covered with brilliants.

"If this goes on, we shall get skating shortly," she said. "What fun!"

"I can't skate," said Polly sadly. "There never was any ice where we lived – not enough for skating, anyway."

"Oh, you'll soon pick it up," said Jo cheerfully.

Meanwhile, the maids were bringing in the big urn of coffee, and the pretty baskets laden with cakes and twists of fancy bread, and the girls gathered round with merry talk and laughter. They were inclined to be drowsy, however, for the hard work of the morning, allied to the warmth of the room and the quiet afternoon they had spent, made them sleepy. Indeed, the four babies *had* slept during the afternoon. From outside came an occasional sharp "cr-r-rack!" as some heavily-laden branch gave way beneath the weight of frozen snow.

Joey nodded her head. "Skating on Monday with any luck! It must be freezing hard now. The windows will be all ice-ferns and flowers in the morning."

"D'you think the lake will bear by Monday?" asked Cornelia. "Those springs, you know – "

"It'll bear all right at the Seespitz end. It's shallow enough there. I don't say it'll bear all over. The frost will have to carry on for much longer than that before it is."

"Why?" asked Polly curiously.

"Don't ask me. I only know that the springs do make a big difference, and no matter how hard or how long it freezes, there are certain parts of the lake that are never safe."

"Jo, do you think we might ask to go to the Dripping Rock tomorrow for our walk?" asked Yvette suddenly. "It must be wonderful now."

"Good idea! It'll be fresh to Polly, and Robin hasn't seen it for years – nicht wahr?"

The Robin shook her black curls. "Not since I have been at the Annexe. I am so seldom down in the winter. Oh, I do hope Miss Annersley will say yes!"

They were talking idly in this strain, when a sudden wild yell from outside startled them all to their feet, making Jo upset her newly-filled cup. As the hot liquid soaked through her skirt, she added to the shrieks that still resounded.

"What is it, then?" gasped Yvette, in her own language.

"Guess it's someone being murdered," announced Cornelia, tearing to the window to drag back the curtains and see if she could see anything.

The rest flocked after her, all except Jo, who suddenly tossed into a corner the handkerchief with which she was

182

trying to scrub her skirt dry, and made for the door. Turning to see what she was doing, the rest rushed after her, with the exception of the little ones, who clung round big Thora, so that she had to stay where she was. She also put out a hand and grasped the Robin as she galloped past her.

Headed by Joey, the others reached the side door where the mistresses were congregated, to find them surrounding one Jockel, a youth who helped in the gardens and attended to the cricket pitches and tennis lawns in season. Miss Wilson had always declared that he was slightly "wanting". At first the bewildered staff were under the impression that "slightly" had become "altogether". He could only grovel there, mouthing at the ladies, and clutching the skirts of Miss Annersley, who happened to be nearest.

"Jockel, cease this nonsense!" she said authoritatively in German. "What does all this mean?"

"The devils – the beautiful white devils!" howled Jockel, crossing himself rapidly. "They rose round me as I entered the snow-lane, mein Fräulein. I have barely escaped with my life!"

"*Rubbish!*" said Miss Annersley trenchantly. "What do you mean? Bring him in, some of you, while I go and see what has upset him."

She was forestalled by Joey, who rushed out, regardless of the fact that she was bare-headed and coatless.

"It's our statues!" proclaimed Jo, standing a little way down the lane. "He hadn't seen them before, and – well, I suppose they *are* rather alarming if you come on them suddenly."

"Jo! Are you mad?" cried Miss Annersley. "Come in at once!"

Suddenly realizing how she was clad, Jo obeyed meekly, and the mistress, having seen for herself that the statues were almost certainly the cause for Jockel's extraordinary outburst, followed her in, and shut the door.

"Go to the staff room, Jo, and wait for me there," she said grimly. "You girls, go back to the common room at once."

Miss Annersley was generally regarded as the gentlest member of the staff. Miss Wilson was renowned for her biting tongue, and Miss Stewart had a peppery Scots temper, while even merry little Mademoiselle Lachenais could be roused to fury on occasion. But Miss Annersley was an equable person as a rule. However, there was a legend in the school to the effect that when she was really roused, she could beat Bill at her own game, and she was obviously roused now. The girls melted out of sight with startling rapidity, and Jo scuttled away to the staff room, shaking in her shoes.

It took the entire staff, the cook, and Eitel, Jockel's immediate overlord, to make the lad see sense. He had known nothing about the morning's "sculping", for he had had permission to set off early to go and see his mother and the new baby brother who had arrived three days before. The place chosen for the statues had been where two of Eitel's lanes met. Poor Jockel, coming by the one from the far gate, had suddenly come upon those hard-frozen images, and in the shock, his scanty wits had deserted him. The light had been streaming over them from the uncurtained staircase window, and, as Miss Annersley herself acknowledged, they had a most ghostly look.

At long last they reduced the lad to something approaching his normal state, and then Miss Annersley left the kitchen regions for the staff room, where she read the penitent Jo such a lecture on taking insufficient care of herself as sobered that young lady for the rest of the evening.

It was nearly time for Abendessen before the school had finally calmed down, and, all things considered, Miss Annersley decided that once that was over, the best thing would be to send everyone to bed. They had had a late night yesterday; and what with the morning's hard work, and the evening's alarms and excursions, the girls ought to be tired out. It would be the wisest thing for Jo, who could not behave madly with impunity. Two years before, she had nearly died from pneumonia, and Miss Annersley had no desire to have that experience repeated.

"Bed – and hot bottles – and warm milk all round," she told her colleagues. "And you might rub Jo's chest, Matron. It's wiser to take no risks."

"I quite agree," said Matron briskly. She paused, mischief in her eyes. "And what about a dose of cod liver oil, Hilda? Jo can't monkey with colds."

The staff rocked with delighted laughter as they pictured Jo's disgust when she was faced with the nauseous draught.

"If *that* won't teach her to stop doing mad things, I don't know what will," said Miss Edwards, when she had calmed down again.

"She deserves it," said Miss Annersley. "Give it to her, by all means, Gwyneth. Perhaps it will make her think twice another time before she rushes out into the bitter cold without enough on her."

Matron chuckled. "And it's all for her own good, too. It shall be done!"

And done it was. Protest she never so wildly, Jo found

that she had to submit to having her chest and back rubbed with Matey's patent embrocation, *and* swallow a generous dose of the hated cod liver oil into the bargain. She stopped her protests when she found that Matron Gould was as determined as ever Matey could be. Besides, the Robin was sitting up in bed, eyeing her with astonishment. Jo choked down the horrid stuff before that look, and then collapsed on her pillow.

"Go away, Matron! I hate you! If there were a society for the suppression of cruelty to girls, I'd report you to it!"

Matron gurgled aggravatingly, and left the room. However, she returned shortly with two very big and comforting bull's-eyes, one of which she gave to Jo, and the other to the Robin.

"That will finish the warming process," she said as she took her departure. "Good night, both of you. I'm going to switch off the light now, and there is to be no more talking."

Jo sat up. "Good night, Matron. All is forgiven between us!" she said dramatically; then dropped on her pillow with a sigh of contentment. Bed was so soft – so warm. And she did love peppermint!

CHAPTER 16

A Fresh Calamity

The school came back on the Tuesday night to find that the Tierntal was veiled with snow, the lake black with ice.

"It looks like an onyx set in crystal," said Polly idly, as she surveyed it from the window of the Yellow Dormitory.

"Are onyxes black?" asked Cornelia. "Say, guess you're something of a poet, aren't you?"

Polly flushed, suspecting teasing, though nothing was further from Cornelia's mind at the moment. "I'm no such thing! But Aunt Mariana had an onyx brooch she always wore, and it was shiny black as the lake is now, and it reminded me."

"Polly, is your case ready?" asked Matey, coming in. "Hurry up, then, and take it over to your own House. We want you people out of the way as soon as possible. Be quick, now! We've trouble enough without your adding to it!" Then she went out again.

At the reminder, Polly flushed again, shoved her possessions into her case, shut it, and went off to St Clare's, very thoughtful and silent.

Trouble had come to the Chalet School indeed.

That morning, Matron Gould, going to see how Mademoiselle Lepâttre was, had found her lying unconscious in her room. Matron had flown for Miss Annersley, and between them they had got her back to bed. They managed to bring her round, but the slightest movement brought back faintness, and, thoroughly alarmed, Matron had rung up the Sonnalpe, and begged that one of the doctors might come down as soon as possible. She also rang up the hotel at Kufstein, where Matron Lloyd was spending the holiday, and asked her to return as soon as she could. Matron Gould was only young, and she was frightened at Mademoiselle's condition.

Meanwhile, Miss Annersley had gone over to St Clare's for Nurse, who came at a run when she heard what had happened. It was a tremendous relief to hear that Matey said she was coming by the next train, and would be at Spärtz at noon. They were to make arrangements to meet her there, and she hoped to be at the Chalet as soon as possible.

From the Sonnalpe came the news that Dr Jem and Gottfried Mensch would both come down at once, and one of them would go on to Spärtz to meet Matey. So, having done all they could, Miss Annersley left Matron Gould with the patient, and went to the girls.

It was a fine day, grey, and bitingly cold, for the frost had the land in an iron grip. But there was no snow, and no likelihood of it before nightfall, if then. The girls were told to wrap up well, take their skates, and go up to the Seespitz end of the lake for the morning. They were safe enough there, and it would get them out of the way. Stacie and the Robin might not skate, so they and Jo set off to walk round the lake to Buchau and back, and Miss Edwards went with them.

It had been hoped that the girls on the ice would be too much absorbed in their sport to notice the Die Rosen car when it came. Unhappily for this plan, someone looked round as the car drove over the crisp snow and recognized Dr Jem at the wheel. There were shouts of welcome at sight of him, and two or three girls came to the edge of the lake, Cornelia and Suzanne among them. They saw the nurse sitting at his side, and Gottfried and another of the Sonnalpe doctors behind.

"Something is wrong," said Suzanne instantly. She stared at Cornelia. "Corney! It is Mademoiselle! She is more ill than they have told us, and that is why we have not seen her at all this holiday."

They had been enjoying themselves, but this finished it. They hurried to take off their skates, and raced back to school with anxious faces.

It was long before they got satisfaction from anyone. Indeed, it was not till Matey, arriving even sooner than anyone had dared to expect, had heard all the news, that they were told anything beyond the fact that Mademoiselle had been taken suddenly worse. *She* promptly declared that the girls had a right to know a certain amount. For Mademoiselle was gravely ill, and already they had phoned for an ambulance to be sent from the Sonnalpe, to where she must be removed.

The doctors declared that they had no idea how she had managed to keep up as long as she had done. She must have suffered more or less continual pain all the term.

"The girls must know," decided Matron. "They all love Mademoiselle, and if – *if* anything were to happen, they would never forgive us for not warning them. Of course, the babies need only be told that she is very ill but I think the older ones should know how serious it is. I don't believe in trying to shield girls from all sorrow and trouble. We want to make strong, helpful women of them – not spineless jellyfish!"

So the elder girls were told that Mademoiselle's life was in grave danger, and that an operation must be performed immediately. She would not return to the school for many months, and they must not look for it.

"It will be a very difficult and dangerous operation, girls," said Dr Jem heavily, when he told them. "We shall do all we can for her, but the final issue must rest in God's hands. You can help her with your prayers, remember. You shall have regular news of her, for I know how anxious you will be. One other thing: the staff will be short-handed for the rest of the term. You can help the school by what you *are*. Remember that the little ones will be watching and following your example. That is all; I must go back to Mademoiselle now. Chin up, all of you! Down-heartedness never helped anyone. Courage has often carried a man to what looked like an unattainable goal."

He left them then, and they went to their own places, very subdued.

Cornelia knelt down by her bed, and buried her head against the plumeau. She was perfectly still, and if anyone had asked her, she would have said that her mind was a blank. A motherless girl, she had had most of her mothering from the two Heads of the school; and in the very nature of things, much of it had come from Mademoiselle. Cornelia had been a firebrand when she came; but the influence of the school had taught her many things, and she knew that she owed Mademoiselle a heavy debt.

Jo, coming to ask her about the Fifth Form work, found her there, and stopped short, feeling intrusive. But Cornelia had heard the light step, and she lifted to the elder girl a deathly-white face, in which her great blue eyes seemed brighter and more enormous than ever.

"Joey," she said.

190

Joey went in, dropping the cubicle-curtains behind her, and sat down on the bed. She laid a slender hand on the square shoulders. "Poor old woman!" she said, her beautiful eyes soft and misty.

Cornelia squirmed till she was kneeling against the elder girl, an arm flung round her waist.

"She's been all the mother I've ever had," she said in muffled tones. "She and Madame between them. I – I guess I feel kind of bad about this!"

Jo smoothed the fair curls that just reached Cornelia's shoulders. "I know. But you heard what Jem said, Corney. We can only buck up as hard as we can. It – we can't think of *us* at present."

Cornelia's shoulders heaved a moment with a heavy sob. Then she straightened herself. "Guess that's all it amounts to," she said, squaring her jaw. "You're right, Joey! I'll play up!"

Wise for once, Jo said no more, but left her to herself, and went back along the corridor, where she met Yvette Mercier, who told her that Miss Annersley wanted her in the study. Jo nodded, and went there, to find a palefaced Miss Annersley busy with the timetable.

"Telephone call from Die Rosen, Joey," she said curtly.

Jo turned to the telephone. "Madge! – what's that? – Just arrived, you say? How has she stood it? – No; I suppose they can't, yet – *What*? – Oh, Madge! That's horribly soon! Will she be able to stand it? – Yes; I suppose it's best to get it over. You'll let us know, won't you. – You know how worried we all are. – Right! We will! Goodbye!" She rang off, and faced Miss Annersley.

"Yes; they are going to operate at once," said that lady gently. "I think we'll have Prayers now, Joey. Everyone has come, I think."

"Babies as well?" asked Jo, as she went to the door.

"Yes; this is something for us as a school. Even the babies shall have their part in it."

Jo hurried away, and presently the sound of feet, moving quietly, came to the study, where the mistress was still struggling with the necessary rearrangement of the time-table. When Miss Annersley entered the common room, she found her flock standing quietly in their places, every face grave, and a strange hush in the atmosphere.

Miss Annersley did not dwell very much on things. She reminded them that their Head was dangerously ill, and that they could help her with their prayers. Then she began, and if her voice shook a little now and then, only the elder girls noticed it.

Prayers over, they were dismissed for Abendessen, and all the younger girls were sent to bed as soon as it was over. The elder girls begged to sit up till news came of how the operation had gone. Miss Annersley agreed, knowing that they were little likely to sleep at present. They could have their sleep out in the morning. She returned to the study and the timetable; Joey made a determined attack on history for the next day; the rest of the staff either struggled with work, or else joined the silent girls in the common room, and tried to keep them from dwelling too much on what threatened. They were soon joined by the others, who found all attempt at work fruitless while their minds were occupied with other things.

Mademoiselle Lachenais had gone up with the ambulance, so that the Head might feel that she had a compatriot with her, and she returned about twenty-one hours, white with grief and fatigue, but very composed. She brought no later news. Mademoiselle Lepâttre had stood the journey as well as they could hope. She had been semi-conscious most of the time. They had taken her straight to the sanatorium, where she had been prepared for the operation at once, and they had just wheeled her into the theatre when Mademoiselle Lachenais set out to return to Briesau.

"Did you see anyone who knew anything?" asked Jo fearfully.

Mademoiselle shook her head. "But no, my Jo. How could I? All thought was for our dear Mademoiselle. I could not disturb them by asking unnecessary questions. Dr Jem will see that someone rings us up when it is over; but that is all."

"They're an awful time about it," said Miss Leslie restlessly. "How long is it since they took her away – five, six hours? It must be something like that."

"They were not quick in going," Mademoiselle reminded her. "The ambulance had to drive slowly. I came down by the direct path."

"Yes; how on earth did you do it?" demanded Jo, thankful for something to distract her thoughts.

Mademoiselle Lachenais held up one foot. "I wore my nailed boots, of course, and I had my alpenstock. Also, there are many stars and a young moon, so that I was well able to see. And I am an Alpinist, as you know. It was not difficult, and that way I could come by myself. To have come down by the road, someone must have driven me; or else I must have waited for the train, and I knew that I might be needed here."

"It was good of you, Mademoiselle," said Miss Annersley quietly, but with deep gratitude in her voice. "But you must be very weary after such a climb. Elsie, go and bring Abendessen for Mademoiselle. Perhaps she will eat it here among us."

"Indeed, I should prefer that," said Mademoiselle.

"Can't I get your slippers?" suggested Jo, rising. "Where are they? Tell me, and I'll bring them. Your feet must be tired in those great boots!"

Mademoiselle smiled. "They are not light, certainly," she agreed. "I should be grateful for my slippers. They are on the little shelf below the window in my room. A thousand thanks, my Jo!"

Jo hurried off, and presently returned with the dainty slippers so characteristic of the little lady, who slipped them on with a sigh of relief, while Evadne removed socks and boots to the kitchen. Then Elsie appeared with the tray, on which was a dainty little supper, and two of the maids followed her with huge trays, laden with bowls of milky coffee for the girls.

Miss Annersley looked her surprise at this, whereupon Trudi explained that Maria thought the young ladies would be glad of a hot drink while they waited for news.

"It is most thoughtful of Maria," said Miss Annersley. "Please tell her, Trudi, that we are very grateful. And say that when any news comes through, I will myself bring it to the kitchen."

Having handed round their trays, Trudi and Gretchen bobbed their curtseys, and went out, and once more the girls settled down to that seemingly endless waiting.

"Oh, will they *never* ring up?" wailed Anne Seymour, when the clock struck for twenty-two hours, and there was still no sign from the Sonnalpe. "It must be *hours* since they began!"

"Not yet three; and they said it would take longer than that," said Mademoiselle Lachenais.

The sound of hurrying feet in the corridor made them all jump with frightened anticipation; but it was only

Miss Wilson, come to report that Miss Stewart, who still knew nothing of the shadow which hung over the school, was asleep. "Is there any news?" she added anxiously.

"None," said Miss Annersley.

"Doesn't Miss Stewart really know yet?" asked Evadne.

Bill shook her head. "No; the doctors say that we are not to tell her till – till we know one way or the other. So she has gone to sleep quite happily. She is much better, I am thankful to say, and looking forward to going home on Thursday."

"Is that when they are coming for her?" asked Jo idly. She knew the answer already; but anything was better than sitting thinking.

Miss Wilson nodded. "Yes; her brother comes for her then, and will take her away at once. Don't let her know anything, girls, for if we can keep it from her, we must. Otherwise, she may try to insist on remaining, and Dr Jem says she *must* have the rest."

"Better not go near her, then," said Jo gloomily. "*I* shan't! I should give it away in a moment if I did."

Silence fell again, and held until the clock chimed for twenty-three hours. Then came the sound of swift feet, and Matey, who had gone to the study for something, entered. There was that about her which told them that she brought news at last; but for a moment she seemed unable to speak. Then she managed it.

"It's over!" she said, a queer croak in her voice. "The operation has been a success!"

"Then go to bed at once, girls," said Miss Annersley, rising quickly, and checking the demonstrations of delight that would have broken forth if she had not spoken. "No noise, please, or you may wake the others. We shall have fresh news in the morning, I expect. Good night, all of you!"

Bill and Miss Nalder promptly shepherded off their own eight, while the members of Ste Thérèse's departed quietly but joyfully. Jo, last to go, shook her head. Living so close to the Sonnalpe, she realized, as the rest did not, that the success of the operation did not mean that all was well. Miss Annersley saw her, and resolved to let her know whatever else had been said before she slept.

"What else, Matey?" asked Miss Leslie when the staff were alone at last.

"The operation is a success, as I told you. But the heart is very weak – they are giving injections already – and – " Matron paused, and cleared her throat.

"And – what?" asked Miss Norman, who had come over from St Agnes' when she had seen her little flock to bed.

"They are not sure how she will stand the shock – well, they are doing all they can, and we can only hope and pray for the best."

No more was said. The staff parted for what was left of the night, looking very grave. Miss Annersley fulfilled her promise to the kitchen staff, telling them that the operation was successfully over. She said nothing more, bidding them get off to bed as quickly and quietly as they could. Then she went slowly upstairs to the pretty room where Joey was kneeling by her window, staring out at the black lake in its frame of driven whiteness. As the mistress entered, switching on the light, she turned her head sharply.

"*Don't!*" she said. "Put that out – I can't bear it just now!"

Miss Annersley obeyed, and then came to sit down on

the broad window seat by her side. Jo lifted heavy eyes to her face. "What else?" she asked.

"Nothing – at present," said Miss Annersley gently. "The heart is very weak; but they hope." She turned and gazed out on the frozen lake for a moment, to give Jo a chance to steady herself. Then she spoke. "Joey, you must go to bed and try to sleep. There will be work for you tomorrow, and you cannot hope to work well if you are tired out. Mademoiselle will have the best of care; and the future lies with God. Remember that, child, and try to trust Him. Now, good night." She took the white-faced girl in her arms, and kissed her – and from Miss Annersley, that meant much. Jo clung to her for a moment. Then she struggled to her feet.

"Right!" she said curtly. "I'll get to bed. Good night, Miss Annersley. Thanks for being so good to me!"

Miss Annersley left her, and went on to Mademoiselle Lachenais, for she knew the merry little Frenchwoman was devoted to the Head. Mademoiselle had had the long, tiring walk, in addition to anxiety and grief, and the senior mistress felt just a little worried about her.

But little Mademoiselle was quite calm. "I shall compose myself to sleep," she said quietly. "That is the best thing I can do. Bonne nuit, ma chère Hilda. Dormez bien!"

"Bonne nuit, ma Jeanne," replied Miss Annersley. "May there be better news in the morning."

Then, mindful of her own advice to Jo, she went to bed too, and did her best to sleep.

CHAPTER 17

Joey Unfolds a Tale

The news from the Sonnalpe continued to be good. Very slowly, but very surely, Mademoiselle came back from the gates of death, and ten days after the operation was performed, Dr Jem rang up the school to say that, humanly speaking, she was out of danger now.

The school received the news with a certain soberness. Mademoiselle's illness had been so sudden, and her danger so grave, that not even the good news of her recovery could make them wildly hilarious. They had always known that they respected and admired her; but many of them had not realized how they loved her till it seemed possible that they must lose her. So, though there were rejoicings, they were tinged with a certain gravity.

"This won't do," said Miss Annersley to the assembled staff the day after the news came. "I know the girls have had a bad fright; but it's time they had got over it. Mademoiselle herself would be the first to say so. We don't want the term clouded. I'm going to call Assembly, and dictate the parts for the Christmas play."

"A good idea," agreed Miss Wilson. "In any case, it's high time rehearsals began. We haven't too much time left, and we don't want this year's play to be a frost when we've always done so well before."

"Agreed!" said Miss Nalder. "What time will you hold Assembly?"

"At half-past fourteen. It's snowing again, so they can't

go out. I'll give out the parts, and they can have the time for learning them. Grace," she smiled at Miss Nalder as she spoke, "if you'd like your dancers, I'll send them to you. They won't have any speaking parts, so you can begin on them at once."

"What about the singing classes?" asked Miss Wilson.

"Too bad for Mr Denny to come out," said the senior mistress quickly. "But, Sarah," she turned to Miss Denny, "you might tell your brother, and ask him if he has the carols chosen. He can begin on them at the next singing lesson."

Miss Denny nodded. "Right! What about the solos?"

"Jo, Corney, Evvy, Yvette, and Stacie. They all go to Mr Denny for singing, so he'll arrange them as he chooses."

"What exactly am I?" asked Joey, who had been sitting quietly in a corner, as befitted the youngest and newest member of the staff.

"You are the Spirit of the Bells," returned Miss Annersley. "The play is called 'The Bells Of Christmas'. Corney is the Spirit of the Snow; Evvy, the Spirit of the Christmas Rose; Yvette will be the Spirit of the Holly; and Stacie the Spirit of Love. You people have very little apart from your singing, so that you will not have much to learn."

Everyone departed, and work began for the day. That afternoon Miss Annersley kept her word. She held Assembly, read out the play to the excited girls; dictated the parts; and before long, the school was hard at work on it.

News from the Sonnalpe continued to be excellent. Mademoiselle would not be able to resume her duties till after Easter, but if she went on as she was doing, the doctors had every hope that she would be able to do so then. Die Rosen was at last declared free from infection, and Jo went up to spend a joyous weekend there as soon as possible.

She was amazed at the difference she saw in her nephews and nieces. Sybil had produced two teeth; little Jack was crawling all over; Primula Mary was blooming like a rose in the crystalline, bracing atmosphere, and looked, as Jo said, pounds better. But those who had been ill were most changed. David, Bride, and Rix were as sturdy as ever, and had all grown. But Peggy looked almost another child. She had lost all her dainty chubbiness, and was very tall and thin.

"Madge," said Jo later on, when the children had gone to bed, and the two were together in the salon, "I'd no idea Peggy had been so ill. It gave me a horrid shock when I saw her."

Madge Russell, slight, dark, with the beauty born of a sweet nature in her delicate face, looked into the big eyes fixed on hers. "Jem wouldn't have you told, Joey; but we came very near to losing Peggy during those two or three days she was so ill. However, she's all right now, and she'll soon be plump again. She's much better already. If you'd seen her as I first saw her, poor little scarecrow, you'd have had every reason to feel shocked."

"But she's such a length!" said Jo protestingly. "She looks far more like six than four."

"She's just half an inch taller than Rix," said Madge. "You don't notice it so much in him because he's so sturdy. You needn't worry, Jo. Jem says that Peg will be all right before long. She's sleeping well – and you saw what her appetite is like for yourself!"

"Yes; she's certainly improved there," agreed Jo.

"And now, tell me all the news," said her sister. "How

do you like teaching? How is that child, Polly Heriot, getting on? Has Biddy O'Ryan told any more banshee yarns this term? And is the Quintette as wicked as ever?"

Jo sighed in an elderly fashion. "The Quintette is sobering down," she said. "Even Corney and Evvy are becoming responsible beings. Oh, Joyce Linton has been distinguishing herself, by the way. Such a joke!"

"What has Joyce been doing?" asked Madge sharply.

"Oh, nothing outrageous. You needn't get so windy. It was only an accident. But it *was* funny – about the one funny thing that's happened this term!" And Jo chuckled infectiously as she thought of it.

"Oh, Jo! Do get on with the story! I could shake you when you sit and chuckle like that!"

Jo slipped further down in her chair, her long legs stretched before her in a most unladylike attitude. "All right; keep cool, my lamb! I'm going to tell you all about it."

She pulled down her skirt, and then began. "You know about Corney's exploit with the garlic when we first began cookery? Well, ever since then, everyone's been almost painfully careful in cooking.

"On Monday, Five A and B had their cookery lesson, and after they had prepared Mittagessen, Frau Mieders, by way of being affable, said they might make cakes for Kaffee – any kind of cakes they liked. They were to do them by themselves, and she wasn't going to interfere at all. She would stay there with them – it was Corney who told me this, by the way – and she would knit. If they were really stuck, they could ask her, but they were to try to do without her if they could.

"So they began. Corney says that she made jumbles; but they got badly singed, so we never saw them. Someone made gingerbread; someone made torte; someone made madeleines – oh, a variety of things.

"Joyce decided to try her hand at Cornish saffron cakes. She had the recipe in a kind of odds-and-ends book she keeps, and as she hadn't expected to want it, she had to go upstairs to fetch it. As it happened, the kitchen saffron was finished, so Frau Mieders told her to get some from Matey, who, it appears, keeps it for her own nefarious purposes.

Joyce got the book, and then hunted up Matey, who was quite amiable, and took her along to the medicine cupboard to get it. Just as she'd unlocked the door, Cyrilla Maurús came along, looking pretty ghastly. She'd slipped with a handful of test-tubes, and cut herself pretty badly. Matey only stopped to tell Joyce to get the stuff from the third tin on the right-hand side of the cupboard, and bring it back when she'd finished with it. Then she marched Cyrilla off to the bathroom, and left Joyce to herself.

"Joyce wasn't sure – in the excitement over Cyrilla – just *what* Matey had said. She opened the tins to make sure, for it was fearfully dark – you know what Monday was like – and Matey's writing isn't the easiest in the world to read. However, she found it at last, and went off with it, after closing the doors, of course. Matey came along just then for lint and bandages, and *she* only glanced at what Joyce had taken, and then let her go.

"Joyce says she mixed her cakes very carefully – she's quite good at cookery, you know, and likes it – and finally had them ready for the oven. It struck her that the saffron looked rather brighter than usual – almost canary-colour, in fact. But she put that down to its being a German product, and thought no more about it. Hers were the last to go in, as she had been rather a long time getting what she

202

wanted, and by the time she had finished, it was time to lay the tables for Mittagessen.

"Frau Mieders had given her the little oven at the far side, so that the cakes shouldn't be interfered with by the others looking in to see how theirs were going, and it was just as well.

"I was teaching the Third – German Dictat, if you want to know – when the most *awful* smell began to creep in. We simply couldn't think what it was. I decided that Bill must be giving the Sixth some extra niffy experiment, and I wished she'd keep the lab door shut. But it got worse and worse. I never smelt anything more awful in my life!

"Frau Mieders wasn't in the kitchens just then, as she'd been called away to the telephone; and the Fifths were busy in the Speisesaal, and didn't notice anything – or so they say.

"Anyhow, it got so bad – really suffocating, you know – that I went out to see what on earth was happening. By that time, Frau Mieders had got through with her telephoning, and she was making a beeline for the kitchens. She got there ahead of me (for by that time, I knew it didn't come from the lab), and I was scooting for there as hard as I could go.

"We got there, and I give you my word that those kitchens smelt as though the devil himself had come to pay us a visit! Half the staff had got there, too; and Nally was opening the oven doors, quite regardless of the fact that she was making most of the cakes into flat failures! She came to the little oven at last, and when she opened *that* door, we were all nearly knocked over! She raked out the patty-pans, and the stink was worse than ever. Joyce landed into the middle of it, and gasped when she saw her cakes spilling over the floor – literally. They weren't cooked enough to be set through. Oh, what a mess there was!

"Finally, Bill and Nally grabbed up the lot, and chucked them out into the snow. Someone opened the doors and windows – we preferred to be frozen, rather than suffocated – and the smell faded away.

"The next thing was to find out what had happened. Joyce vowed that she'd put in nothing but what the recipe had said, and it must be the German saffron. Then Bill had an inspiration. She took Joyce by the shoulder, and marched her upstairs to find out from Matey what it was the kid *had* used, while Frau Mieders began closing doors and windows, and the Fifths bewailed their spoiled cakes. Naturally, letting in the cold like that chilled the ovens, and most of those cakes gave it up and sat down flat!

"As far as I can gather – I had to go back to my babes then, for they were making row enough to raise the roof by that time – Matey unlocked the cupboard, produced the saffron tin, and opened it. Joyce looked inside, and said it wasn't the one she had used – Madge Russell! If you giggle like that, you'll choke! – I suppose you can guess what came next? That wretched child hadn't used saffron at all. She'd taken the *sulphur* tin, and flavoured her cakes with *that*! Matey blames herself for not giving Joyce the tin with her own hands; but as we all told Joyce, if she couldn't tell the difference between saffron and sulphur by this time, she ought to be ashamed of herself!

"Poor old Joyce! She won't be allowed to forget this in a hurry! I'm going to give her home-made sweets for Christmas, and they shall be in a sulphur-yellow box – they shall, if I have to make it myself! – *and* I shall write 'Sulphur Delights' across the lid!"

Madge Russell laughed till the tears ran down her

cheeks at this latest exploit of the girls. She could well imagine the smell there must have been when that sulphur began to warm up! As for Jo's threatened gift to Joyce, she put a stopper on that. Joyce was a touchy young person, and she would certainly flare up over such a joke. Jo groaned derisively at the mention of Joyce's temper, but said no more about the matter. Not that the idea was wasted. Cornelia and Evadne had evolved it on their own, and the result was that among her Christmas gifts, Joyce received a lemon-yellow box containing fondants and marzipan, all bright yellow in hue, while across the bottom of the box was written, "In memory of the latest recipe for cakes."

The post came just then, and Mrs Russell distributed the letters at once. Jo took her share of the letters, Miss Annersley having handed them back to the postman with the intimation that Miss Bettany was at Die Rosen, and he had brought them up with the rest. There was one from Frieda Mensch, full of news of the latest addition to the family. Another came from lovely Marie von Eschenau, who had formed part of the quartet which had ruled the school so wisely for a year. Jo sat and chuckled over this, for Marie was to be married after Christmas, and the letter contained a full account of her trousseau, as well as describing the bridesmaids' dresses. Jo was to be chief bridesmaid, and Frieda and Simone Lecoutier (Mademoiselle Lepâttre's young cousin, now at the Sorbonne in Paris) would be the other two; so the letter was full of interest to Joey. Next came a long letter from New Zealand, where lived the former maths mistress of the school and her husband. The last of the batch, a typewritten envelope, the young lady had tossed aside as uninteresting. But when she had finally concluded all the letters from friends, she took it up with some curiosity.

"Who on earth's sending me typewritten letters?"

"Open it, and then you'll see," suggested Madge, without looking up from her own mail.

Jo turned it over, glanced incuriously at the monogram on the back, and then slit it open. A typewritten sheet dropped out, and she unfolded it, wondering what it could be. Two seconds later, Madge was startled into a violent jump by a wild yell from her sister.

"*Joey!* What on earth is the matter?" she demanded. Then she dropped the letter she was holding, and sprang to the girl's side. "Jo! What's wrong? Tell me this instant!"

Jo raized dazed black eyes to her face. "*Oh*, Madge! Oh, *Madge!*"

"Joey, what *is* it? Tell me at once before I shake you!"

"Oh, Madge!" Joey was stammering in her excitement. "It – it's from those people I sent *Cecily Holds the Fort* to. Madge! They *like* it – they say so! They say their reader has reported favourably on it! And they offer me thirty-five pounds for the copyright! Think of it, Madge! *Thirty-five pounds!*"

Madge plucked the all-important letter from Jo's fingers, and read it for herself. It was brief and businesslike, but it brought joy to her, for it meant that her sister had set her foot on the first rung of the ladder. Where it might lead her, no one knew. But Madge felt that no other letter could ever give her quite the same thrill.

As for Jo, she seemed positively awe-stricken. At first she could only sit in a dazed silence, holding her letter, which she had grabbed back at the first possible opportunity, and looking – as Madge declared later on when she was retelling the whole story to Jem – as if she had been offered the Crown of Britain and a huge fortune at one and the same time. Presently the words came bubbling up as Jo felt her sister's kiss of congratulation. "Madge! My first book! I'm a real author!"

"I know! Oh, Joey-baba! How proud I am of you! Oh, how I wish Mother and Father had been alive today to know about it!"

Joey laughed a little. "I'd forgotten about them. I suppose it's never having seen them. I always feel as though you were my sort of mother, you know. You've brought me up, after all."

Madge Russell, with a thought for the long-dead parents, nodded. "I know. But – don't forget them, Joey. They would have been so proud of you."

"Yes; but it's scarcely the same as if I'd known them. Oh, I don't forget them, of course. Only – they're rather – strangers."

"Who are?" asked Dr Jem, coming into the room at that moment. "Hello – post! Anything for me, dear?"

"Over there on the table. But never mind about them for the moment, Jem. Just listen to Joey's news!"

Jem turned to his young sister-in-law. "What is it, Joey?"

For reply, Joey thrust the letter into his hands. "Read that, Jem! Oh, Madge! I simply *can't* believe it's true!"

After a sharp glance at her excited face, the doctor read the letter through. Then he dropped it, picked up the tall, slim girl, and kissed her heartily. "Well done, Joey! This is splendid news! I'm as proud of you as I can be; and as for Dick, I'm going to send him out a new hat of extra large size, for I'm certain he'll need it!"

"Isn't it gorgeous?" Joey clung to him. "Oh, Jem, I'm so thrilled!" And then the reaction came, and she burst into tears.

She was soon all right again, however, and able to settle down and discuss the news quietly.

"What will you do with your money when you get it?" asked Jem.

"I'm going to buy presents for you and Madge and Dick and Mollie. And I'm going to buy something for myself for a memento. And the rest I want to send to Vater Stefan for his poor children. You don't mind, do you, Madge? I have so much, and I'd like to feel I could do something like that with it. It's my *first* earnings, you know."

They both knew what she meant, and they agreed. "Only little things for us, though, Joey," said Madge. "We'd love to have something in remembrance of today, and of course, we'll have the book. But don't spend much on our things. And I think it's a very good idea to send your first fruits to Vater Stefan. Don't you, Jem?"

He nodded. "Yes! But Madge is right, Joey. You mustn't waste your money over us."

So it was decided. Jo finally provided new fountain pens all round, and bought a new book she herself had been wanting; but the greater part of the cheque when it came – and when it had been duly cashed – went to Vater Stefan in Innsbruck to provide a summer outing for the children of his parish. It was very thrilling; but, as a matter of fact, Jo was far more thrilled when the following October brought out to the Sonnalpe six copies of her own book, beautifully illustrated, with a gay paper jacket which was warranted to attract any schoolgirl.

That, however, was almost a year ahead. At present, Jo, after an evening of wild hilarity, retired to bed with the promise that on the morrow she would be permitted to see Mademoiselle for five minutes.

It was scarcely a social call, that visit, for the visitor was very nervous, and all she did was to grin at the Head, say "Hello! Hope you're all right!" and then slip out.

But when she returned to the school, she was able to tell the girls that Mademoiselle, though very thin and white and weak, was still their Mademoiselle.

After that, she had to announce her own news, at which the school went rampant, and if she had given away all the copies that were promptly demanded, she would soon have become bankrupt. She finally got them away from the subject by demanding to know what had been done about the play while she was absent, and in the excitement of telling her, they forgot other things for the time being.

The rest of the term was divided between lessons, rehearsals, and work for the big boxes they were filling for Vater Stefan, and which rejoiced his heart exceedingly when he opened them. They were crammed full of toys, clothes, and everything the Chalet School could think of that children might need and they supply. Other gifts rained down on the young priest as well, for the colony at the Sonnalpe had heard of what was going on, and insisted on bearing their part.

Finally, Cornelia's father sent a cheque to provide firewood for the winter for as many families as possible. And Mr Lannis, not to be outdone by his friend, added a further sum to give them other comforts. So that, all things considered, one parish in Innsbruck had cause to bless the Chalet School that Christmas.

CHAPTER 18

The Christmas Play

The days fled past so quickly that it seemed to the girls as if they had just begun to rehearse the play, when the dress rehearsal was over, and the actual performance itself was on them.

On the day of it, Vater Stefan came up to Briesau to meet his benefactors. What they had expected, none of the girls were very sure, but it was certainly not what they saw. He was quite a young man, dark and slight, with smooth black hair, and a pair of magnificent grey eyes, which glowed as he thanked them for their goodness to his people.

"Be very sure that the dear God will bless you all this Christmas," he said, as he tried to show them his gratitude.

Then the gong sounded for Mittagessen, and Miss Annersley bore him off to the staff table, while the girls formed into long files and marched into the Speisesaal.

Once the meal was over, they had to disappear, for all had to dress. Vater Stefan went off with the doctors who had come down, to have a quiet pipe and chat in the library until it was time to go into Hall. They found him, like most Benedictines, a highly educated, cultured man, who, though he often longed for the peace of his monastery, where he might study and know privacy, was quite content to labour among his poor people in obedience to his Abbot.

"And what a fröliches Weihnachtsfest they will have this year!" he said joyously.

"Are you people here?" asked Miss Nalder, peering round the door. "You must come now, for the doors are opening, and we want Vater Stefan to have a good seat."

The hall was filled to its fullest capacity, and the little orchestra, composed of various members of the staff, began to play the Bach Christmas music. Presently the music ended, and the curtains were drawn to show a chilly-looking room, with ten great golden bells swinging a little above the stage. Suddenly, from the glockenspiel, played by Herr Laubach, came the sound of twelve strokes, and on the last one, the black curtains at the back of the stage parted, and a tall, slim figure in flowing draperies of gold appeared – Jo.

She advanced amidst an intense silence, and then, to the lovely air played by the strings and woodwind of the orchestra, she sang a carol which was new to everyone. Madge had written it, and Mr Denny had composed the music. Softly Jo's lovely voice began; but as she reached the last verse, it swelled up and out, filling the great hall:

> Ring out, ring out, oh, Christmas bells
> Ring out your tale of joy and mirth.
> Bid man forget his fruitless strife
> This night – the night of Jesus' Birth.
> This one night of the year, oh, world,
> Bid strife depart, dissensions end.
> Oh, world, give love from man to man.
> And with the bells your anthems blend!

Then came the chorus:

Ring out, sweet bells, oh bells of gold
That sing of Love that cannot cease!
Join in, ye bells of silver mould.
Your tale of Christ's eternal peace!

Softly chanting, "Ring out – ring out – ring out!"
the Spirit stood in the centre, and on the last sweet note,
the music from the glockenspiel rang out gaily, and down
from the golden mouths of the bells tumbled sprites clad in
gold and silver, who caught hands, and danced gaily round
Jo.

At length, the music ceased, and the little spirits fell
back in a tableau, while the Spirit of the Bells spoke to
them, bidding them, one by one, speak of the place to
which their music had brought a special message. The
violins whispered soft notes on the last word, and the
curtains fell.

The choir broke into another carol, the very old German "In dulci jubilo", which ended just as the curtains
were raised, to show a richly furnished bedchamber of
the fourteenth century. A lady clad in robes of the same
era sat at the spinning wheel, and in the bed lay a child
– the Robin. Maids were busy about the room and the
little maid in the bed. The lady – Anne Seymour – left
the wheel, and came to bend over the child, and ask if she
could give her anything. The child said there was nothing
she wanted. She was only waiting to hear the Christmas
Bells that would speak of the Birth of Christ.

"I know I shall be well when I hear that," she said.

The maids clustered round, one offering to tell a tale;
another to sing; the third proffering her cup. The child
put them all aside. She was listening for the bells. Suddenly, a strain of soft music stole out. Gradually, the

restless people on the stage fell asleep. Then, through the curtains, drifted a form clad all in white, frosting on gown and hair, and a crown of silver on her head. It was the Spirit of the Snow. The sick child sat up and held out her arms. But Snow shook her head. She had brought a gift; and standing there, she sang the carol of the snow – again verses of Madge's set by Mr Denny. Cornelia had a charming voice, and she sang very tenderly the little carol with its soft chorus of "Lullay lullay". The bells chimed in with her singing – this was an effect in every one of the solos – and the sick child slipped back against her pillows and fell asleep. Suddenly, the bells rang out in a soft peal. The grown-ups started awake. Their first thought was for the child. They bent over her; the mother's glad voice spoke the message.

"She sleeps at last! The bells have sung her to sleep, and now she will recover! And this is Christmas Day!"

At once the curtains fell. The school choir sang behind the scenes the pretty old English carol "On Christmas Day in the Morning".

Again the curtains swung back, this time on a miserable garret, cold and cheerless. Three ragged children were there, barefoot and unkempt; and a white-faced woman who wept because it would be Christmas Day tomorrow, and they could have no share in it. Even, they might be without a roof, for if the landlord should come for the rent, they had no money to pay him.

The children tried to comfort her; but she refused their comfort. Then the youngest said, "But we can share the bells, liebe Mutter, for they belong to everyone!"

The next one cried, "Hark! I hear the bells now! Christ is born!" And at once came the faint chiming of the bells.

Another voice sounded, singing with them; and Evadne, the Spirit of the Christmas Rose, entered, surrounded by a throng of smaller roses. They filled the stage, passing to and fro, and hiding the poor family as they moved. Evadne, standing well forward, sang the legend of the Christmas Rose, which tells us how, at the first Christmas, a little beggar-girl wanted to enter and offer a gift to the Babe of Bethlehem, but had nothing, until the Archangel Gabriel appeared to her, and showed her a great bank of white flowers, the first Christmas roses to grow on earth, and bade her take those to Him, for God had given them to her.

Evadne's song finished; the little roses swung back; the bells rang out a merry peal in a changed room. The chilly blue lights had become warm amber; the poor people were neatly and warmly clad; food stood on the table; and in one corner was a Christmas tree, all lit up, round which the children gathered joyously.

Again the curtains fell, and again the choir sang – an old Angevin carol, known to the French as "Quoi ma voisine?"

They rose this time on a darkened stage, to which people presently came limping, as if they had walked a long way. They carried bundles, and staves, and big lanterns, for they were gypsies, and were tramping to find a site for their camp. They told of the long journey over the wintry roads; the sharpness of the bitter wind; the chill of the snow. They were so tired, so cold, so hungry. And then the Spirit of the Holly danced in, all in green and scarlet, and bade them camp where they were, for this was the place chosen for them to keep their Christmas. Yvette had a charming mezzo-soprano voice, and she sang her little song very sweetly. The people sat down. Some

214

of them produced sticks for the fire, and electric torches switched on under scarlet paper gave a fine glow, while the light was changed from blue and green to crimson. At once the bells rang forth, and the scene was hidden, while the choir sang the Czech carol "Hajej nynjej", or, as it has been translated, "Little Jesus, sweetly sleep".

The fourth scene was a king's court, with courtiers, jester, and dancing girls all complete. A great number of the girls appeared in this scene, and in their gay dresses they made a brilliant picture. It was plain that the king had returned from some great victory, for presently captives were brought in, heavily chained. They knelt down at the king's feet and begged for mercy. He frowned, and refused it. They had been his enemies, and they must suffer for it. Suddenly, the bells rang out again, and the Spirit of Love floated in, clad in long, rose-coloured draperies. Hers was a very short carol – only two verses, for this was Stacie's first public appearance. But she sang it very clearly and sweetly. The king's attitude slowly changed as she sang, and he made a gesture, at which the guards flung off the chairs from the captives, and they were free.

Down came the curtains, and while the choir sang the Welsh carol "O, deued pob cristion", which may be translated, "All poor men and humble", there was a deep hush on the audience.

Then the curtains parted again, to show the room in the bell tower, the Spirit of the Bells standing in the centre, the little bell sprites about her, while the Spirits of the Christmas Rose, the Snow, Holly, and Love knelt before her.

Joey spoke, softly but very clearly, and with deep feeling.

215

Now ye have heard the stories of the Bells.
Now do you know that when their music swells
It bears a message unto every heart;
It reaches through the world to every part.
And that ye ne'er forget the tale they sing,
That they their joy and peace to you may bring,
Look now upon the scene that, long years past,
Was shown to man amidst the winter's blast.
We have them still – the Cave, the Manger Bed;
And still the silent stars shine overhead.
Down to the earth, drifted on sleeping wings,
The herald angel still his message brings
Of love and peace, goodwill from man to man.
See but the scenes, and then, forget who can!
While o'er the earth those joyous anthems steal,
And in the tower the Bells of Christmas peal,
Here is a King, a wanderer poor, a Child,
An Artisan, a Mother, humble, mild.
Oh, Bells of Christmas, ring – ring out all strife,
And sing to us of Him Who gives us life!

She ceased, and the curtains closed, while the choir sang
the old Swedish carol "Congaudeat turba fidelium". As
they finished, the glockenspiel chimed in once more with
joyous pealing, and once more the stage was shown. This
was the hillside at Bethlehem, with the "shepherds abiding
in the fields, keeping watch over their flocks by night." To
one side, and poised above them, were a throng of angels,
clustered together. This part of the stage was flooded with
rose and amber light, while the rest was in shadow, so
that the eye was swiftly led to the angelic choir. For a
few minutes the audience saw it in silence. Then it was
blotted from their sight by the curtains.

But almost at once, they were swung back to show the Three Kings – Melchior, Caspar, and Balthasar – bearing their gifts of mystic meaning, while above them swung a great silver star. Slowly they came forward, one after another raising the gifts to show what they had. Melchior swung chains of gold; Caspar swung a censer; Balthasar raized a white flask.

Then, even as they turned to go on their way, the curtains came down, and when they were lifted, it was on the Stable in Bethlehem.

Angels clustered round the central group, in which St Joseph – Thora Helgersen – stood protectingly behind the Madonna – Louise Redfield.

For the last time the curtains fell, to rise on the same place. But now the angels crowded to the back, while at the feet of the Madonna, who stood holding the Bambino, were the shepherds and the kings. The various characters from the other scenes were grouped at the sides, and at either end of the wooden trough, which was in the centre, with St Joseph still behind it, stood the Spirits, only the Spirit of the Bells standing beside St Joseph.

Almost simultaneously with this, the glockenspiel rang out in a very ecstasy of joyous music. The orchestra chimed in; the music changed; and the sound of the glorious old Latin hymn, "Adeste Fideles" rang through the previously silent hall. The audience joined in singing it, the curtains fell and the play was ended.

"The most beautiful thing of its kind I have ever seen," said old Mr Wilmot, who had come to take Polly home to England for the holidays. "I – upon my word, my glasses need cleaning!" And he took them off and polished them.

"A tale that can never be stale nor too often told," rejoined Vater Stefan, a deep glow in his eyes. "I wish my children might have seen this. They could never forget then the Gift which Christmas brought to the world."

Joey, still in her flowing robes, was standing near when he said this. Her eyes suddenly lit up. She turned, and moved away to where Miss Annersley and Miss Wilson were standing speaking to Stacie Benson's uncle and aunt, who had come from Devonshire to escort her to their house for the holidays – the first time she would see England after nearly two years. The Stacie who had left them had vanished, and the girl who was going back was one they would be delighted to have with them.

Jo spoke to them prettily, and then contrived to draw the two mistresses away to a corner, where the Robin, still in her loose white gown, presently joined them. For a few minutes they talked together earnestly. Then the Robin slipped across the room to where Vater Stefan was standing, and put her hand in his.

"If you please, will you come?" she said shyly. "Miss Annersley and Miss Wilson and Joey want you."

Greatly wondering, the young priest let her lead him to them.

As they went, he looked down into the lovely little face at his elbow, and smiled. The Robin smiled back, and squeezed his fingers.

"It is Joey's thought," she told him eagerly, "but Miss Annersley and Miss Wilson say yes. It cannot be at Christmas, for everyone will be at home then. But when we come back – *then*!"

Wondering what she was talking about, Vater Stefan halted before the group in the corner. Then – he could scarcely believe his ears. For in addition to all their previous kindness, they were offering that when the girls returned from their holidays, a hall in his district should be hired, and this beautiful little play should be given there for the benefit of his poor people.

It was as much as Vater Stefan could do to stammer out his thanks. It was so unexpected; and he knew what it would mean, this spot of colour and loveliness, in the grey lives of those among whom he so faithfully laboured.

Later on, he recalled the Robin's mysterious words, and before saying goodbye, he sought Joey out. "Mein Fräulein," he said abruptly, "I can never thank you for your so-beautiful thought. But the prayers of my church will follow you always. May God bless you!"

Joey looked at him. "When we have so much," she said slowly, "isn't it only fair that we should share all we can with those who have so little? Isn't that the message of Christmas, mein Vater?"

He smiled. "Ah, yes! But how many think of it thus?"

"Ah, but we are taught to do so," said Jo gravely. "I must go, Vater Stefan; they are calling me. Auf wiedersehn. Fröliches Weihnachtsfest!"

She ran off, scarcely waiting for his farewell, and was at once surrounded by a throng of girls, all begging her to come back next term, and go on teaching them.

"Not likely!" said Joey calmly. "My book is accepted, and I've got to start a new one – Well, of course, I shall! Think I'm going to stop short now? Oh, I'll come down to see you – often. But as a regular thing, I really have finished with school now. There's Jem calling me: I must go! Goodbye, everyone, and a happy Christmas to you all!"

She wriggled free, raced to the car, and sprang in. Dr Jem started her, and, waving her hand, her eyes not so clear as they might have been, Joey drove away from the Chalet School.

Enid Blyton books have sold millions of copies throughout the world and have delighted children of many nations. Here is a list of her books available in paperback from Armada Books

First Term at Malory Towers
Second Form at Malory Towers
Third Year at Malory Towers
Upper Fourth at Malory Towers
In the Fifth at Malory Towers
Last Term at Malory Towers

The Twins at St Clare's
The O'Sullivan Twins
Summer Term at St Clare's
Second Form at St Clare's
Claudine at St Clare's
Fifth Formers at St Clare's

1. The Mystery of the Burnt Cottage
2. The Mystery of the Disappearing Cat
3. The Mystery of the Secret Room
4. The Mystery of the Spiteful Letters
5. The Mystery of the Missing Necklace
6. The Mystery of the Hidden House
7. The Mystery of the Pantomime Cat
8. The Mystery of the Invisible Thief
9. The Mystery of the Vanished Prince
10. The Mystery of the Strange Bundle
11. The Mystery of Holly Lane
12. The Mystery of Tally-Ho Cottage
13. The Mystery of the Missing Man
14. The Mystery of the Strange Messages
15. The Mystery of the Banshee Towers

ARMADA

The Chalet School Series
by Elinor M. Brent-Dyer

Elinor M. Brent-Dyer has written many books about life at the famous Alpine school. Follow the thrilling adventures of Joey, Mary-Lou and all the other well-loved characters in these delightful stories, available from Armada in 1989:

Gay Lambert at the Chalet School
The Chalet School in the Oberland
Bride Leads the Chalet School
Changes for the Chalet School

ARMADA

STEVIE DAY SUPERSLEUTH
(that's me!)

I'm on my way to being the first female Commissioner of the Metropolitan Police. It's true I have a few personal problems: for a start I'm small and skinny and people are always mistaking me for a boy. I'm 14 – though you wouldn't think so – and my younger sister, Carla, not only looks older than me but she's much prettier too. Not that that really matters. You see, she doesn't have my brains.

If you want to see my razor-sharp mind in action or have proof of my brilliant powers of deduction then read about my triumphant successes in:

STEVIE DAY: Supersleuth
STEVIE DAY: Lonely Hearts
STEVIE DAY: Rat Race
STEVIE DAY: Vampire

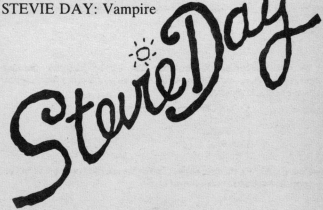

ARMADA

Armada Gift Classics

An attractive collection of famous children's stories which would make ideal gifts. Beautifully illustrated with striking jackets, these books are an essential addition to any library.

Some of the older, longer titles have been skilfully edited and abridged.

Little Women Louisa M. Alcott
Peter Pan J. M. Barrie
Lorna Doone R. D. Blackmore
What Katy Did Susan M. Coolidge
The Wind in the Willows Kenneth Grahame
The Secret Garden Frances Hodgson Burnett
The Railway Children E. Nesbit
Kidnapped Robert Louis Stevenson
Gulliver's Travels Jonathan Swift
The Adventures of Tom Sawyer Mark Twain

To order direct from the publishers just tick the titles you want and send your name and address with a cheque/postal order for the price of the book plus postage to:

Collins Childrens Cash Sales
PO Box 11
Falmouth
Cornwall
TR10 9EP

Postage: 60p for the first book, 25p for the second book, plus 15p per copy thereafter to a maximum of £1.90.

ARMADA

Have you read all the "Secrets" stories by Enid Blyton?

THE SECRET ISLAND

Peggy, Mike and Nora are having a miserable time with unkind Aunt Harriet and Uncle Henry – until they make friends with wild Jack and discover the secret island.

THE SECRET OF SPIGGY HOLES

On a holiday by the sea, Mike, Jack, Peggy and Nora discover a secret passage – and a royal prisoner in a sinister cliff-top house. The children plan to free the young prince – and take him to the secret island.

THE SECRET MOUNTAIN

Jack, Peggy, Nora and Mike team up with Prince Paul of Baronia to search for their parents, who have been kidnapped and taken to the secret mountain. Their daring rescue mission seems doomed to failure – especially when the children are captured and one of them is to be sacrificed to the sun-god.

THE SECRET OF KILLIMOOIN

When Prince Paul invited Nora, Mike, Peggy and Jack to spend the summer holidays with him in Baronia, they were thrilled. By amazing luck, they find the hidden entrance to the Secret Forest – but can they find their way out?

THE SECRET OF MOON CASTLE

Moon Castle is said to have had a violent, mysterious past so Jack, Peggy, Mike and Nora are wildly excited when Prince Paul's family rent it for the holidays. When weird things begin to happen, the children are determined to know the strange secrets the castle hides . . .

Armada